Penguin Books
The Umbrella Tree

Rose Zwi was born in Mexico, lived in London and Israel but spent most of her life in South Africa. Her previous publications include *Another Year in Africa*, *The Inverted Pyramid* and *Exiles*. She has won several prizes for her work in South Africa.

In 1988 Rose emigrated to Australia and now lives in Sydney. She is married and has three children.

Rose Zwi

The Umbrella Tree

Penguin Books

Assisted by the Literature Board of the
Australia Council

Penguin Books Australia Ltd
487 Maroondah Highway, PO Box 257
Ringwood, Victoria 3134, Australia
Penguin Books Ltd
Harmondsworth, Middlesex, England
Viking Penguin, A Division of Penguin Books USA Inc.
375 Hudson Street, New York, New York 10014, USA
Penguin Books Canada Limited
2801 John Street, Markham, Ontario, Canada L3R 1B4
Penguin Books (N.Z.) Ltd
182–190 Wairau Road, Auckland 10, New Zealand

First published by Penguin Books Australia, 1990
10 9 8 7 6 5 4 3 2 1
Copyright © Rose Zwi, 1990

Typeset in 12/13 Perpetua by Midland Typesetters, Maryborough
Made and printed in Australia by Australian Print Group, Maryborough

National Library of Australia
Cataloguing-in-Publication data:

Zwi, Rose.
The umbrella tree.
ISBN 0 14 013410 7.
I. Title.
SA823.3

Creative writing program assisted by the Literature Board of the Australia Council, the Federal
Government's funding and advisory board.

For the children of Africa

GLOSSARY

Amabhulu Zinzinja!	The Boers are dogs!
baas	boss
blackjacks	members of the African municipal police, so called on account of their uniform
Blue Ribbon dress	Blue Ribbon is the brand name of a well-known flour which used to be sold in large cotton bags
boetie	brother
bush	low indigenous shrubs which intersperse the grass of the veld, often of a thorny or scrubby nature
chatas	derogatory term for a non-Jew, coming from the Hebrew word for sinner
chech hymn	church hymn
cosmos	type of plant
dassie	rock rabbit
Great Trek	Migration from Cape Colony northwards, from 1836, of Boers dissatisfied with British rule and the abolition of slavery
ground-nuts	same as monkey nuts or peanuts
ja-baas	yes boss

kaffirs	means of address or reference to a black person, regarded by both black and white South Africans as offensive
knobkerrie	a fighting club or stick usually with a knobbed head
koppie	a hillock, common feature of the South African veld
kraal	an enclosure for farm animals, surrounded by wattle or thorn tree branches staked into the ground and lashed together with wire
kwela-kwelas	police pick-up vans
laager	encampment of wagons lashed together for protection of people and animals within. Figuratively, a protective environment usually in a political sense signifying an ideologically impenetrable enclosure
location	black township
mealies	maize, indian corn. Extensively cultivated and used in numerous forms in South Africa, e.g. mealie meal a finely ground maize meal which is the staple food of most of the black population of South Africa. Also stamp mealies, used like rice
mme	mother
mokgotse	friend
mopane	shrub or tree sometimes called ironwood. An important fodder tree in low rainfall areas
morgen	area of land, about 0.810 of a hectare
muti	African medicines, spells and herbs

ngaka a tribal doctor using both herbal medicines and tribal spells in the treatment of disease. 'Horned doctors' diagnose by throwing bones

office police station

platteland literally, flat lands. Rural areas

shebeen an establishment in which illicit home-brewed liquor or other liquor is sold without a licence usually by African women known as shebeen queens

stoep terraced verandah in front of house

toktokkie a large black beetle of the genus Psammodes. Its mating call, tapping of the ground or floor, is often mistaken for a knock on the door

veld open country, neither cultivated nor true forest or bush

vetkoek a cake usually made of yeast dough, deep-fried and similar to an unsweetened doughnut

Viva Azania Long live Azania. Azania is the name used by many blacks for South Africa. 'When our people are planning . . . a revolt in any country the first thing they do is to alter the country's name. So Rhodesia is known as Zimbabwe, South-West Africa as Namibia and South Africa as Azania.' (Credo Mutwa, *Dictionary of South African English*.)

voetsek a rough command to be off – usually to a dog. Offensive if applied to a person

vokenbastard A well-known vulgar expression translated into Afrikaans. 'V' in Afrikaans is pronounced as 'f'

waai literally blow – fly, dash away

ware pronounced vaara – Afrikaans for true

ONE

Joseph crouched behind the mealies, watching the car ↑
along the rutted road. As the late morning sun reflect↑
off its surface, obscuring shape and size, he shielded ↑
eyes against the glare. From that distance the vehicle cou↑
be anything from a Volkswagen to a wire-windowed polic↑
van. Except when there was a wedding or funeral, car↑
were a rarity in the village. Only donkey carts, tractor↑
and an occasional bus used the road.

He looked back to the bottom of the mealie patch.
From there he could push through the spindly plants
whose cobs were drying between tattered leaves, climb
over the wire fence into their neighbour's plot, and walk
through the sunflowers that stood as high as a man this
season, towards the stream in the valley. The best trained
dogs, Alex had assured him, lost a scent at the water's
edge. Despite heavy summer rains, the stream now ran
slow and shallow. It would be an easy wade upstream to
the village, to the house Alex had shown him.

As the car drew nearer, Joseph shivered. It couldn't be
Alex; he only came at night. Six weeks after Alex had
brought him home from Soweto, Joseph had heard a car
stop outside the house, a door close quietly, then their
pre-arranged whistle: three long notes in a descending
scale. Joseph had slipped into the moonless night, careful
not to wake his grandparents and young brother. He found
Alex near the umbrella tree. That time he had shown
Joseph the house in the village. When he had come again,

four months later, he told Joseph to lie low a while longer; it was not yet safe to leave. Two months had passed since that night. Joseph longed to go to the house in the village, but Alex had stressed: only in an emergency. Anxiety, Joseph supposed, was not an emergency. Neither was boredom, nor the desire to be doing things other than tend his grandparents' small mealie plot. He kicked a stone angrily. Patience was an older-generation virtue.

Joseph breathed more freely when the car turned off the road onto a path no stranger would have found. It lay concealed in the tall pink-tipped grass and led to the three homesteads on the outskirts of the village: his grandparents', Phineas', and Koko Ramasela's. The road itself flowed on to the village, its sandy tributaries leading to other, almost identical smallholdings, where baked-mud houses stood in dusty yards. In the mottled shade of their umbrella trees, the villagers gathered to talk, while scrawny chickens darted about, pecking among parched bushes and plants. Only the old and the very young lived in the village. Most able-bodied adults worked either in the towns or on the farms of the Boers.

Few people grew sunflowers or ground-nuts; water and labour were scarce. Those who still owned cattle – his grandparents had sold theirs long ago – kept them in a kraal near the house, and every day the young cowherds drove them to the common grazing ground at the far end of the village.

Joseph only went into the village when he took Sammy, his younger brother, to the clinic. The village had not changed since he had left it at the age of twelve. The butcher, the builder, the general dealer and the shebeen queen had houses of brick; the rest of the people lived in mud houses, and like their chickens, scratched out a meagre living from the soil.

There were not many public buildings: a clinic, the corrugated-iron church of the Methodists, the wattle and daub Dutch Reform Church, and the brick church of the Roman Catholics. In the battle for souls, the Catholics had had an edge on the other churches for many years, but now the people were flocking to the black syncretists, the Zionists, who gathered on the banks of the river every Sunday, dancing and singing ecstatically in praise of both the Lord and their Ancestors. In death they were united in the common graveyard that lay at the far side of the grazing land.

Bordering on the grazing land was the school the grandmothers had built. Joseph remembered being carried on Dikeledi's back every day to the building site where his grandmother worked with the other women of the village. They drew water from the well, mixed sand with concrete, then poured it into oblong moulds, all the while keeping a watchful eye on their grandchildren who played under a large tree.

It had taken two and a half years to build the school. When the June unrest had erupted the previous year, rumours reached the village about school burnings. His grandmother and the other women had converged on their school with brooms, knobkerries and sticks. They drove out the children, who were boycotting lessons in sympathy with students in other parts of the country, then kept an all-night vigil at the gates. Only government property is being burned, the students assured the women. Reluctantly the grandmothers went home. But when a veld fire broke out later that week, they again rushed to the school's defence.

Joseph turned from the mealie patch and walked towards the house.

'Mme!' he called as his grandmother came into the enclosed yard carrying a bundle of dry wood. 'I'll gather the wood.'

'And who does it when you're not here?'

'While I'm here, I'll do it.'

She put down the wood and shading her eyes, looked towards the road.

'There's a car stopping outside Ramasela's house,' she said.

Through the long grass Joseph saw three women, two white, one black, get out of the car. The black woman opened the creaking cat's cradle gate, and walked towards the house.

'It's Anna,' Dikeledi said. 'She's come to visit her mother and her children but there's nobody at home. Ramasela will only be back this evening. All that way from Johannesburg. I wonder who brought her?'

'Her kind madam, no doubt.' Joseph picked up the wood and walked into the kitchen, a three-sided structure at the back of the house with a roof of corrugated iron. In the centre of the kitchen was a concave plate of iron where the ashes of yesterday's fire still lay. Next to it was a three-legged pot caked with congealed mealie meal around which flies were buzzing. A large box stood in one corner, neatly piled with cooking utensils, wooden spoons, enamel plates and mugs. In the other corner was a covered bucket with a long rope attached to it. Joseph lifted the lid and scooped out a mugful of water. His mouth was parched and dry.

'Where's grandfather?' he asked Dikeledi, aware as usual of the absurd nomenclature. He called his grand-mother Mme, mother; her husband Sello he called Ntate Mogolo – grandfather. His mother, when he saw her, he called either Ellen or ausi – sister. There was no one he called father. Would the day ever come when black children would know whom to call father? Joseph scooped another mugful of water out of the bucket.

'He's down at the vegetable garden with Sammy, picking the beans. Have you started to gather in the mealies?'

'Only the very dry ones. There's still time. The rains are over and they'll come to no harm. This afternoon I want to dig a new well. The old one's running dry. I'll have to dig it nearer the river this time, but it will be further for you to walk.'

Dikeledi shrugged. 'Another few yards won't matter. It's difficult enough to drag my swollen feet from the present well. You'll have to fetch the pick from your uncle Benedict. He took it the other day to make another sewage pit. Poor Benedict.' She sighed as she walked into the house. 'Poor Benedict.'

TWO

Uncle Benedict. Malome Benedict. Ever since Joseph could remember he had worn that army trenchcoat, buttoned to the neck, his hands thrust deeply into the pockets. Only his bloodshot eyes, wrinkled forehead and white, pot-scourer hair emerged from the turned-up collar. Summer and winter he trudged through the veld, gesticulating and mumbling to himself. The only words he was ever heard to utter were, 'Beware the forked lightning. The night of the fires is coming.'

Benedict had joined the South African Defence Force during World War II and spent eighteen months in Tobruk and Egypt as an ambulance driver; blacks were not allowed to carry arms. Nobody knew what happened Up North, but he returned a changed man. Shell-shock, some said; blighted hopes, said others. Soldiers had been told they were fighting for a better life, a just society. White soldiers got housing, blacks got trenchcoats.

Benedict had moved out of his parents' house and built himself a corrugated-iron shack at the far end of their plot where he lived like a hermit. Dikeledi left food and occasional items of clothing at his door but never went inside. He would disappear for weeks, prophesying fire and destruction to the unheeding veld and bush. The villagers left him in peace.

Soon after his return, Dikeledi had travelled to her home village, about a hundred miles north, to consult her uncle, a 'horned doctor' who threw bones. The prognosis had been bad: the Ancestors are unappeasable, the uncle told Dikeledi. Benedict has fought on the side of the enemies who stole our land and oppressed our people. He should have kept himself for the real battle which will not be long in coming.

Benedict could have been a great ngaka himself, Dikeledi often said to Joseph. He had the gift, the vision.

The only beings with whom Benedict had any contact were animals and children. Joseph had been a particular favourite. As a child he had sat silently outside his uncle's hut, watching Benedict carve animals out of wood with a penknife, his other heritage from the army. Before Joseph left the village to go to school in Johannesburg, Benedict had kissed him, put the knife into his hand and said, 'The night of the fires is coming. Beware the forked lightning.'

When Joseph returned home a few years later, Benedict had turned away from him; he had grown up, become a stranger.

Dikeledi came out of the house and, with a dry-grass broom she had made herself, swept the courtyard. How old and frail she looked, his Mme. Joseph rubbed his eyes; the dust made them smart. She and Sello had had a hard life and suffered heartache from their children.

Only once, after the death of her son Pitso, had Dikeledi shown Joseph her grief. One and a half children left from seven, she said, crossing her arms over her withered breasts. Benedict, after all, is only half a person. As a child he was bright and healthy, she told Joseph, but the next children were born in bad times. Two died at birth and the third died of measles at the age of two. When the fifth child was born we named her Nkatsana, kitten,

7

in order to deceive the evil spirits into thinking she was an animal; they snatched human babies away. The spirits had been fooled for nearly twenty years. When Nkatsana went to Johannesburg to work as a domestic servant, she met a man who seduced then abandoned her. She died in Baragwanath Hospital after trying to abort her pregnancy.

Then there had been Pitso, so named because he was born during a great gathering in the village. He was the quiet, steady one who worked in a factory near Pretoria. Mmapitso everyone called her; mother of Pitso. He took his leave every October when the first rains fell, and came home to plough the land and plant the mealies. He lived with his wife and four children in Mamelodi. One Christmas he came home on a visit with his family. Phineas, their neighbour, gave a party at which two men got very drunk and started a fight. Pitso was stabbed to death when he tried to separate them. Now I'm no longer Mmapitso, Dikeledi had said. There's only your mother left and poor Benedict. She and Sello were respected in the village: they had borne adversity with dignity and restraint.

Dignity, restraint, humility, Joseph muttered angrily as he swept the ashes from the concave plate with an impatient gesture. The Christian virtues. He crumbled up some paper, put the wood Dikeledi had gathered over it, and reached for the matches. A nation of tame kaffirs with a ja-baas mentality and a turn-the-other-cheek religion, that's what we have become. But not for much longer. He watched the paper ignite and the flames lick the dry branches. That era is passing rapidly.

It was from Dikeledi that Joseph had learned the lore of his people. She told him about Modimo, the creator of all things, who also controlled the weather. He sent wind, hail and heat, and withheld the rain if his people departed from their ancient customs. He was a remote god, approached mainly through the ancestral spirits, and Joseph had difficulty visualising such a being. Not so with Dingwe, the cannabalistic ogre who haunted his childhood dreams. Dikeledi had brought back special charms from her uncle to protect him against Dingwe. The Ancestors, on the other hand, were part of everyday life. It was they who were invoked when the crops failed, when there was illness in the family or when Modimo withheld the rain. They were the benign intermediaries and Joseph had always felt at ease with them.

Best of all Joseph had loved her folk tales. His favourite was about the defeat of the monster Kgodumodumo, who had descended on a village and swallowed up all the people and their cattle. Only one expectant mother had escaped by hiding in the bushes. She gave birth to a son, Senkatana, who grew into a vigorous young man within hours of his birth, and who then killed the monster, liberating his people and their cattle.

'When I grow up,' Joseph used to tell Dikeledi, 'I will change my name to Senkatana, slay the monster and make my people free.'

His long maturation period had been a constant source of frustration to him.

Only Alex, whose return he was so eagerly awaiting, had been as great an influence on Joseph as his grandmother.

'Joseph!' she called out to him. 'We are getting visitors. The car's coming here. Put some chairs under the umbrella tree and boil up the water for tea.'

THREE

As Louise stepped out of the car into the long grass, the ants swarmed over her feet. She brushed them off with quick nervous strokes.

'We should have worn stockings,' said Freda, her mother-in-law, stamping her feet.

'It wouldn't help, madam, they eat stockings also,' said Anna as she opened the gate. 'The ants are hungry in this village, like the people.'

There was no sign of life from the house. It's like a child's drawing, Louise thought, leaning against the gate: a corrugated-iron roof held down by large stones, two unmatched windows set into sloping mud walls, and just off centre a blue door which creaked and swung back as Anna opened it and disappeared into the dark interior. 'Mme! Abram! Willie!' she called as she walked through the echoing house.

'Nobody is here,' she said when she came out. 'It is Sunday. Maybe they have gone to church.' She sounded doubtful. 'My mother, she doesn't go to the church, only when somebody dies, when somebody is married. She always says, too much churches.' Anna laughed. 'She likes only the Ancestors and Jesus Christ, not the churches. We can go to Dikeledi, our neighbour. She knows everything in this village.'

Louise looked at Anna with interest, as though seeing her for the first time. There was a quiet confidence in her voice, she looked taller, and she moved as though she were carrying a fragile object on her head. Since they had left Johannesburg earlier that morning, a subtle shift had occurred in their relationship. As Anna moved onto home ground, she shed her role as servant and treated Louise and Freda as her guests, not her employers.

Louise had always been an uneasy employer, and Anna had played on her guilts. When things ran smoothly she called her Louise; when she was angry she called her Madam. There had been no confusion of roles with Freda. Anna called her Madam and they got on very well.

Anna had taken control as they approached a garage at the turn-off on their way to the village.

'It is better to use the toilets here,' she had said. 'Our lavatory at home is different.'

And although it was only eleven-thirty, she had suggested having lunch before they reached the village. 'There is too much hunger at home and our food is not enough for everybody,' she said.

They had stopped in the shade of a thorn tree opposite an enormous field of sunflowers.

'Like a thousand suns,' Louise had marvelled, putting on her sunglasses.

'The heads are heavy heavy,' Anna commented. 'The farmer will have plenty money this year. My father, he worked on this farm, for two shillings a day, six days a week, twelve hours every day.'

Louise felt a twinge of guilt. She wondered how much her brother paid his labourers. 'He should've taken another job,' she said.

'The other farmers paid worse. And my father, he had five children, so what must he do?'

'In the old country,' Freda said, 'the peasants also had it hard. But after the Revolution . . . ' She smiled re-assuringly at Anna.

Anna had shrugged. She had little faith in Freda's revolutions.

Louise had felt more relaxed after their picnic lunch. They had left Johannesburg early that morning to visit Tony at Pretoria Central. It had been a tense and depressing visit. When they were escorted to the visiting room, he was already standing behind the slatted-glass partition, like an irate postmaster who had mislaid his rubber stamp. The warders seemed more alert than usual.

'What's new in the outside world?' Tony asked Louise after greeting his mother with forced cheerfulness.

'Not allowed to speak about news,' the warder on his side mumbled.

'That was a form of greeting,' Tony said coldly, 'not a question.'

'Everything's fine,' Louise said, then hesitated. 'Hasn't Peter been to see you?'

'He's coming tomorrow.'

She would have to tell him. Not that he wasn't expecting it, but he never gave up hope. He was always petitioning, lodging requests, querying prison procedure, insisting on his rights. It was this, among other things, that had kept him sane during the fourteen years of his imprisonment. It had also made him one of the most hated of the political prisoners: they hadn't been able to break his spirit. She had diminished him with her postmaster image. Would her ambivalence never be laid?

'It's been refused,' she said.

He was silent for a moment. Then he resettled his glasses on the bridge of his nose. 'Predictable,' he said. 'On what grounds?'

'The old story of rights and privileges. Peter put up a strong case when he submitted the application.

Imprisonment was the punishment, he said. A blanket ban on news was mere vindictiveness . . . '

'Not allowed,' said the warder on her side.

Louise apologised in Afrikaans though Tony hated it when she appeased them. Over long years of visiting she had learned to pack her sentences with as much information as possible, then apologise gracefully for overstepping the mark.

'Peter will give you the details,' she said. 'What have you been reading lately?'

'Prison literature.' He smiled grimly. 'There's been progress, it seems. A subtle move from punishment of a man's body to that of his deviant soul. In 1757 a French would-be regicide, Damiens, had his flesh torn from his breast, arms, thighs and calves with red-hot pincers. Then molten lead and boiling oil were poured into the wounds. Afterwards he was drawn and quartered by four horses and his remains reduced to ashes . . . '

'Enough!' Freda had paled. 'You shouldn't give them ideas.'

'It was a public spectacle,' Tony continued. Louise hated it when he baited his mother. 'The crowds loved it. A quick death, in such sentences, showed God's mercy, thus giving everyone a glimpse of justice both on earth and in hell. It also gave them the opportunity to mock authority . . . '

Before the warder could intervene, Freda said, 'My son the philosopher. Don't you even inquire about your sons?'

'Of course, mother. How are my sons?'

'Don't ask.' She shrugged. 'Karl's still – there. But he writes regularly. He's waiting to move – further away. And Freddie is still meditating, burning incense and eating grass – not that kind, vegetables – and he gives away all his things to people who need them more than he does, which is plenty of people. But they're well, bless them. The evil eye shouldn't harm them.'

She turned and spat three times, in the direction of the warder.

Louise flushed and nudged Freda gently; Tony's face had become a taut mask. Freda was growing increasingly tactless. It was the longest half-hour visit Louise had endured for some time.

They were silent as they drove away from the prison. Anna had waited for them in the car, wrapped in her own sorrows.

'Another two weeks before I see Tony,' Freda had said, 'and I always say the wrong thing, I know. All I really wanted to do was to reach out and touch him, to soothe the lines from his forehead. I haven't touched him for almost fourteen years . . .'

She cried quietly into her handkerchief, then blew her nose resolutely. Louise envied her her emotion. It was a long time since she had wanted to reach out and touch Tony.

She glanced out of the window. The rust-tipped grass rippled in the breeze, and the veld looked like a furry beast, crouching, quivering, limbering up for the attack. Flat-topped trees hung over the road, casting pools of shade. The first cosmos, harbingers of winter, were already blooming in the high grass, and swallows were gathering on the telephone wires all along the road. How, in this sultry air, could they tell that winter was approaching? Their forked tails drew patterns in the air as they swooped over the veld then soared skywards, flexing their flight muscles for the long journey over Africa, to the uncertain spring on the other side. How could they bear to leave this beauty, the golden warmth? They were not of Africa but would come again with the spring. But what of those who were of Africa? Those who had migrated unseasonably? They too would return – with fire.

Louise opened the window and the velvet-textured smell of the sweet-thorn flower flooded the car, together with the smell of dry grass and dust.

An endless stream of dun-coloured trucks came towards them as they drove northwards. Soldiers returning from the operational zone, she guessed. As a young girl she had knitted socks and scarves for the soldiers Up North – Tobruk, Abyssinia, Egypt – who were fighting in the 'just' war. The boys on these trucks looked incredibly young with their short hair and sunburned faces. Her brother's sons might be among them. Karl might have been. And who knew what Freddie's fate would be. They drove towards the village in silence, each woman ensconced in her own sadness.

'Before we go to Dikeledi, come see my mother's house,' Anna said.

'What a lovely smell,' Freda said, as she followed Anna across the sandy yard in which only one tree grew.

'It is the flowers of the músú, the umbrella tree,' Anna told her. 'But they are dying now, the summer is nearly finished.'

It was cool and dark in the house. They walked into a small room which had a table, six chairs, a kitchen-dresser and a display cabinet without the glass. Six curtained cubicles hived off from the main room, three on each side of a passage that led into the backyard.

Louise sat down on a rickety chair, leaning her elbows on the table. The beaten earthen floor was uneven and the table rocked a little under the pressure. She looked around the room, recognising cast-off furnishings and household goods she had given Anna over the years: curtains, cups, plates and other dishes; a warped frying pan, a kettle, and some faded shantung cushions. Their drabness filled the room with reproach.

On the sideboard lay a packet of candles, two enamel candlesticks, matches and a porcelain ballet dancer who had lost an arm. A picture of Jesus on the cross hung on the wall. His brow was pierced by a crown of thorns and bright red blood spurted from his wrists and ankles. His face was deathly green, matching the cloth that hung limply around his loins. Another picture showed the resurrected Jesus effortlessly carrying an enormous cross. Dimpled cherubs were draped into the folds of his voluminous blue and gold gown.

Louise got up to read a framed certificate which hung next to the door. It was a removal order granted to Afro Funeral Undertakers of Alexandra Township, to take the body of Thys Modise, aged seventy, from the Natalspruit Hospital to the Doornkloof cemetery. The cause of death was given as cardiac failure, malnutrition, pellagra and hypoproteinaemia. It was signed by the assistant District Registrar of the hospital. Louise herself had taken Anna's comatose father to the hospital two years ago.

She lingered over the other photograph which stood on the sideboard. Mojalefa, Anna's oldest son who must have been about two years old at the time, was sitting on his father's shoulders, with his soft, dimpled hands around Charlie's face. Louise had never seen Charlie so proud, loving and happy before. Nor so sober.

Mojalefa had been a beautiful nine-year-old when Anna had come to work for Louise almost ten years ago. There was only a few months difference between him and Karl, and they had become good friends. Mojo, as Karl called him, spent most of his school holidays at the house and earned pocket money by working as a caddy. Karl once went with him, but was chased away by the other black caddies. He was inconsolable.

'They called me a white vokenbastard,' he had said tearfully. 'And just because I'm white they won't let me be a caddy.'

'My brothers and sisters have all got a room in my mother's house.' Anna drew aside a curtain to reveal a windowless cell which barely accommodated a bed and a few suitcases. 'While my mother lives, this is our home. She looks after our children. When she dies I must come here and look after the children because I am the oldest. The others will sit in the town and send me a few rands when they remember.'

But Louise knew that Anna had other plans; she was a resourceful woman. She had needed to be with six children to support and no help from her drunken husband Charlie. Some years ago Anna had dragged him off to the Bantu Commissioner's Court. The children are all his, she told the Commissioner, and he has never supported them. He's always drunk, a shame to his family. Drink is the sin of my nation, she had added piously. The Commissioner had placed an order on Charlie's wages and every month Anna had collected the sixty rand he earned as a clerk. She gave him fifteen rand for transport, cigarettes and beer. Otherwise he'll run away, she had told Louise. Fifteen rand a month could not slake Charlie's thirst, however, and one day he disappeared. No one had seen him since the previous winter, but every few months Anna received a money order without a covering note, in an envelope postmarked Rustenburg.

To supplement her wages, Anna had sold boiled eggs and vetkoek to the caddies who worked on the golf course on Saturdays and Sundays. It had paid well until other black women entered the market. When competition became too keen, Anna went into textiles. She bought seconds from a knitting factory and clothed the neighbouring domestic servants in irregularly-shaped sweaters and cardigans. But that market was soon saturated. Louise only learned about her third enterprise when she was woken by screams late one night. As she and Freda rushed into the backyard, a stream of people emerged from Anna's room and disappeared into the dark. After some questioning and much evasion, Anna admitted to running a shebeen.

'Why should Charlie buy his drink from Auntie Gladys next door?' she said defiantly. 'If he wants drink he can pay me for it. And when I buy drink for him, I buy for some friends, not for people in the street. Tonight there was trouble because there was a police spy.'

'Drink is the sin of my nation,' Louise quoted bitterly.

'How can I support six children on seventy rand a month?' Anna had replied, hitting her target with unerring accuracy. Louise raised her wages by ten rand and never brought up the subject again. The backyard shebeen flourished, even after Charlie fled.

Anna's febrile attempts to make money were closely tied to her plan to circumvent her fate as the next matriarch of her family. Three of her children lived with her mother, and two were at a mission school in the northern Transvaal. Mojalefa, for whom she had held such hopes, was missing. She wanted to build her own house in a township near Johannesburg, and move her children into it. They ranged in age from eleven to seventeen, and would be able to fend for themselves. She planned to visit them regularly and ensure they had enough to eat and went to school. In this way she would relieve her mother of caring for her boisterous boys, and ensure that her siblings took responsibility for their own children. She wanted to be a mother, not a matriarch.

Anna went into the backyard again, calling 'Willie! Abram! Peter!' There was little point in calling out Mojalefa's name; both she and Anna suspected he was too far away to hear it. 'There's no one here for sure,' Anna said. 'Come, let us go to Dikeledi and Sello. They will know where everybody is. And Sello can tell you some stories about our village. They have been here a long, long time.'

They got into the car again and Anna directed Louise along the hidden path which led to Dikeledi's house.

FOUR

A tall woman with a scarlet scarf tied low over her forehead came slowly towards them. The straps of her square-toed shoes, rigid with age, did not reach the buckles over her swollen feet. She wore a faded pinafore over her open-necked blouse, under which Louise could see the corrugations, like those of a well-worn country road, of her chest. Above her jutting collar bone, a pulse rose and fell unevenly. Her face, except for deep creases at the side of her bright eyes, was unwrinkled.

'I am happy you are here,' she said as she opened the gate. 'Please come to the tree. The sun it is very hot.' Her words of welcome ended on a wheezing cough.

'You speak English,' Freda said. 'I'm ashamed to say I don't know any Bantu language.'

'Before I marry,' Dikeledi said shyly, 'I work for English people five years. They teach me but now I forget. My husband, Sello, he knows English. He is now coming from the fields.'

'My English isn't so good either,' Freda shrugged. 'After nearly fifty years in Africa, I've still got a Russian accent and I still count in Yiddish.'

Dikeledi looked puzzled but smiled, acknowledging the desire for communication. She led Freda to a chair under the umbrella tree.

Louise envied Freda's effortless transcendence of race, language and other cultural barriers. She felt as relaxed with the Indian fruit vendor and her Italian neighbours, as she did among the black people with whom she worked. It's simple, Freda told her. Tony loves the masses, you love the poor and the oppressed, and I love people. No theories, no guilts, no nothing.

State officials were a notable exception; they obviously did not rate as people with Freda. She'd had a running battle with them for fourteen years. After Tony's trial she had shouted, 'This court is illegal! Recuse yourselves! You do not represent the majority in this country!'

On her first prison visit she had spoken Yiddish to Tony, much to his confusion, Louise's embarrassment and the warders' ire.

'I not speaka de English,' she told the prison commandant when she was summoned to his office.

'You speak English,' he told her curtly. 'You made yourself very clear in court. And you'll either speak English – or Afrikaans – to the prisoner, or you won't be allowed to visit him.'

Her English improved remarkably by her next visit. 'Pity,' she said to Louise, 'I could've passed on so much information to Tony in Yiddish.'

'But Tony hardly understands Yiddish,' Louise said.

'Necessity's a good teacher; he'd have learned.'

She never gave up trying to keep him informed, delighting in her cryptic messages which Tony rarely understood. Indeed, was all he answered, looking puzzled and irritated.

'They'll stop your visits,' Louise warned.

'They wouldn't dare. Imagine the headlines: Dying mother – who isn't dying? – prevented from visiting only son in jail.'

She's grown fat, Louise thought as they sat down under the umbrella tree. Freda's legs barely reached the ground, and her heavy buttocks flowed over the sides of the chair. She had always been plump, but since her retirement two years ago, she had put on more weight. I've always wanted to re-read the Russians, she had said, and proceeded to work her way from Pushkin to Solzhenitsyn with the same speed and gusto as she devoured Chocolate Logs, Lunch Bars and Peppermint Crisps. But she had baulked at the social realists. They're bores, she said. Who cares how many bales of wheat a socialist hero produces in the Ukraine? Politics is one thing, literature another. Tony should hear you, Louise said. Freda had shrugged.

She soon tired of her sedentary life, but jobs, at her age, were difficult to get. Louise knew she could not manage on her pension. Move in with me, she told her. Freda demurred. You're young, she said, and have your own life to lead. But when Karl left for Botswana and Freddie moved into a commune in Crown Mines, she came to live with Louise. Shortly afterwards, she was offered a part-time job in the trade union's library.

'Saved,' she had said. 'I was about to eat myself to death, let alone die of boredom among the social realists.'

'Tell me, Dikeledi,' Freda was saying, 'where is that singing coming from?'

'Next to the river the Zionists pray and sing to God every Sunday.'

'Do you also pray at the river?'

'Me, I'm from the Methodist Church,' Dikeledi said, laughing.

'Yes, yes. Like I'm from the Yeoville Hebrew Congregation. But I haven't been to shul for thirty years. What I mean is, do you believe in Jesus Christ and all that? Or do you believe in the old religion of your people?'

Louise flinched. Freda had met the woman five minutes ago and was already enquiring into her religious beliefs. Dikeledi laughed again and offered them tea.

'Don't go to any trouble,' Louise began.

'We'd love some,' Freda said. 'But sit a while. There's so much I want to know.'

A barefoot old man in torn overalls appeared from the back of the house. He was carrying a large sack over his shoulder and was followed by a boy of about ten who carried a smaller bag. The child was coughing. The old man smiled at them shyly, then spoke in Tswana to Anna.

'Sello says excuse me,' Anna translated. 'He did not know visitors were here. He was picking the beans and is not dressed nice. He will come back soon.'

Anna and Dikeledi spoke to one another in Tswana for a while.

'Dikeledi says my mother is gone to Hammanskraal to visit her sister and only tonight she will be back. My children are somewhere in the village, she doesn't know where. No one has seen Mojalefa. But Dikeledi's grandson, Joseph, is here and maybe he knows something. They went to school together, Joseph and Mojalefa. I will go to the mealies just now to speak with Joseph.'

'Tell me,' Freda said to Dikeledi, impatient at the interruption. 'How do you plant the fields? Have you got oxen, a tractor?'

'No oxen. The cattle is too much trouble.' Dikeledi told them that they had sold their cattle long ago. The children sometimes neglected them and they wandered into the fields of neighbouring white farmers who kept them until 'damages' had been paid. And sometimes the farmers themselves chased the cattle into their own fields, then demanded money for their return. 'Too much trouble, the cattle,' she said.

Her son Pitso used to hire a tractor and do the ploughing. Now they hired a man who owned a tractor to do it. This summer their grandson Joseph had helped them but usually she and Sello sowed, weeded, hoed and harvested the mealies themselves. She held out her thin, calloused hands.

'When I go to my ancestors,' she said, 'I will take also my hoe. They will see I have worked too much.'

'So you do believe in the old religion,' Freda said. 'It makes more sense than ours. We have this old Bookkeeper up there, keeping accounts: one sin, one punishment, sometimes more. You don't get a chance to explain, to defend yourself. But with family, you make allowances, especially if they're dead. I worked with this man, Mofolo, for many years in the trade union. He explained things to me about your religion. He also got me muti from the township doctor to help my arthritis . . . '

Oblivious of the noonday heat, of the slow-moving flies that circled their heads, and the frenetic ants at their feet, Dikeledi and Freda began to talk medicine.

'My grandmother,' Freda said, 'used to let blood with leeches when the temperature was high . . . '

'My uncle the doctor,' Dikeledi told her, 'he knows to make good medicine for witched peoples. In the night he digs the roots . . . '

'We've all got our witches,' said Freda. 'And the evil eye. You mustn't say good things about anyone without also saying "no evil eye" and spitting three times . . . '

' . . . when the woman chicken she cries like a man chicken, be careful,' Dikeledi warned. 'Also when there is ring around the moon, be very careful . . . '

'Cut finger nails,' Freda advised, 'should be burned . . . '

It didn't seem to matter to the women that they did

not understand one another's remedies and recipes; what counted was that they had them and believed in them.

The old man reappeared wearing dark pants tied about the waist with a twist of rope; a white shirt frayed at the collar and sleeves, and a pair of black shoes without socks, fitting mates for his wife's shoes: misshapen, wrinkled, laceless. His clothes were probably some white's cast-offs, the rope belt, perhaps, his own.

He was a slight man, much shorter than Dikeledi, who stood up and brought him a rusty paraffin tin to sit on. He shook hands first with Freda, then with Louise. His hot dry palms felt like the sloughed-off skin of a snake. The few teeth he had were embedded in unhealthy-looking pink gums, and his sparse grey beard matched the hair on his head. When he smiled, which was often, his whole face creased into radiating wrinkles. His left eye, Louise noticed, was almost entirely clouded over. He drew out a small tin from his pocket, put a pinch of snuff onto a lightly-clenched fist then, with great satisfaction, sniffed it into each nostril in turn.

'We are happy you have brought Anna to her home.' He laughed. 'She is a good child and does not forget the old people. But she has not come home for a long time, many many months.'

Anna said something in Tswana and he laughed even more heartily, slapping his left thigh repeatedly. Nobody translated that remark.

'My Madam wanted to know about our village,' Anna said in English. 'I told her you were the oldest . . . '

'The Captain is the oldest,' Sello said, giving credit where it was due. 'He was born in January 1900. I am born in October 1901. In 1925 we came here to Vogel-struispan. Together.'

25

'Did you learn English at school?' Louise asked him. This caused a fresh outburst of hilarity.

'No school on the farm where I was born,' he said, wiping his eyes. 'Only cattle school. The children looked after the cattle and the sheep. Mrs Weinstein, she teaches me English. I will tell you about Mrs Weinstein.'

'Ntate Mogolo, tell them the story of our people,' Anna urged.

Dikeledi stood up. 'I go make tea,' she said to Freda. 'Sello, he tells too much stories. Sello is too old.'

'Ho! Dikeledi is too young,' Sello retorted. 'I am born in 1901 and she is born in 1904. But she is too young. Only I am old, nè, Dikeledi?'

She waved him away and walked slowly into the house. The little boy who had been in the fields with Sello was sitting on the front door step. He had washed and was now wearing a pair of clean khaki shorts. His thin shoulders were hunched up and when he coughed, he held his head between his hands.

'The child is sick again, Ntate Mogolo,' Anna said. 'Have you been to the clinic with him?'

'That clinic,' Sello clucked angrily. 'Joseph walks two miles with him on Tuesday and the doctor is already gone. He comes, he goes, and the people wait and wait.'

'Sick chests,' Anna explained to Louise. 'It is in the family. Ntate Mogolo, I will speak with Ellen and she will bring the child to the city. There they will help him.'

'In the city they speak with two mouths,' Sello said contemptuously. 'When you show the money, they say it will be well. Then they say the child cannot live.'

'You and Koko Dikeledi are living, Sammy will also live,' Anna comforted him. 'But he must go to the doctor. I will speak with Ellen. Has she been home lately?'

'Not from the time we planted the mealies. But she

26

is a good girl. Every month she sends money,' Sello said in a subdued voice. Then he spoke in Tswana, in a high-pitched voice. Every now and again Anna clucked sympathetically.

'So now, Ntate Mogolo, you tell about our village.' Anna stood up. 'I go to look for Joseph. Maybe he knows about Mojalefa.'

'Hau, these children.' Sello sighed. He was quiet for a while. 'The Madams really wants to know about Vogelstruispan?'

'Oh yes,' Freda said, drawing nearer.

Sello laughed and closing his eyes, began to speak. His tale was familiar. Louise had heard similar ones from the black people on her father's farm. Hearing it again provided a perverse kind of comfort: black power, it seemed, was as brutal as white power. People, regardless of colour or culture, seemed to break their strongest taboos and committed the foulest acts in order to survive. This knowledge, somehow, spread the guilt a little, making her own easier to bear.

'My grandfather's father was born in Makapanstad, in the time of Shaka,' Sello began.

Louise knew the history of this period. There had been widespread chaos with the rise of Shaka's kingdom. During the 1820s, ancient chiefdoms and old settlements were destroyed, new groups were formed and dissolved, and everywhere disrupted communities fled before the Nguni and Sotho invaders.

'It was too dangerous to walk by yourself,' Sello said. 'No food, no nothing. The fields they are burned, the mealies are stolen. Our cattle are taken away and killed. And the people,' he lowered his voice, awed at what he was about to say, 'they eat each other.'

Louise knew this was no metaphor. She had read that

27

during the Difaqana, the period of forced migrations, the demoralisation and starvation among the people had been so great, that they had finally preyed upon one another and there had indeed been widespread cannibalism.

Those Africans who survived the Difaqana organised themselves under such chiefs as MaNthatisi, that formidable woman; Moshweshwe; Mapakane and others. But before they could consolidate these new configurations, another invader appeared on the scene: the Afrikaner.

Enter my ancestors. Louise wished they had remained in the Netherlands after fleeing from France when the Edict of Nantes had been revoked. Instead, about two hundred Huguenots came out to the Cape to work for the Dutch East India Company in the seventeenth century. And the persecuted, she used to say to her father, became the persecutors. It's not true, her father argued angrily. We fought to survive. Survival, survival! she had shouted at him. In the name of survival the worst crimes are committed.

'My people did everything to live,' Sello said apologetically. 'But that was before they knew Christ.'

Oh Sello, bloody wars have been fought over the centuries in the name of Christ. Don't you know about the massacres, the pogroms, the persecution, the inquisitions? Louise leaned over and patted Sello's hand.

'They had a very hard life,' she said. 'I have just read a book about the Second World War. The German soldiers during the siege of Stalingrad were said to have eaten their dead in order to stay alive themselves. And there was that plane crash, not so long ago . . . '

But Sello's eyes were closed and he was recalling the stories his father and grandfather had told him. After the disruption of the Difaqana, the scattered black tribes were surrounded by the victorious Afrikaners. Some tribesmen became vassals of the Boers; other joined African chiefs who tried to re-establish a separate life as far away from the whites as possible. Sello's family, weary of attacks, migrations, starvation and insecurity, had been among those who became labour tenants on a white man's farm.

'My people were too frightened of the Boer commandos,' he told Louise and Freda. 'The grandfather of my father, he does not know guns. Lightning of the hands, he says; sticks that make thunder. Hau!' Sello laughed, ashamed of such ignorance. 'And when the commandos come to his kraal on their horses, he takes his family and runs. After many days he comes to Frikkie de Wet's farm near Warmbaths, and asks for work and a place for his family. My father is born on that farm, I am born on that farm, many many people in this village are born on that farm. But Frikkie de Wet got many sons and when he dies, the farm is smaller and smaller. The land Baas Frikkie gives to us is taken away and there is no place for our cattle and our kaffir corn. In 1925 we come to Vogelstruispan.'

Louise remembered the labour tenants on her father's farm. They had lived in ochre mud huts roofed over with sheets of iron. The huts were not visible from the farm-house stoep; her father liked unblemished vistas. In return for their labour, the adult men had been given food, limited grazing and ploughing rights, and were paid a small monthly wage. The women who worked as domestic servants were given food and an even smaller wage, while those who worked part-time in the laundry or in the dairy, earned very little. All of them worked on the small plots allotted to them. Boys over twelve herded stock or led the ploughing and wagon teams, and the girls helped their mothers.

You would have not been permitted to enter my father's house, Sello. The tenants stood in the backyard, battered hats in hand, waiting to present their pathetic petitions to the Baas, who believed he was a just man. No one was ever beaten on his farm; they were paid their miserable wages promptly, and he did not even fine them when their children, instead of giving service when they were old enough, left the farm for the city. So just was he, that he even permitted them to return, if they could not find employment in the cities, and did not punish them for running away. Johan Marais, in his own estimation, was a righteous, honourable man.

'When I was so small,' Sello said, holding his hand about two feet from the ground, his fingers touching loosely in an upward direction, 'I was looking after the sheep. No time for school, no time for playing. But sometimes we play and forget the sheep, they are lost and we are beaten. Ai, ai, ai,' he laughed ruefully, 'I cannot forget. My father has strong hands. He looked after Frikkie de Wet's farm very nice.'

Early every morning, Kleinhans, her father's 'coloured' foreman, drove Louise over rough, corrugated roads in the cattle truck to the primary school in Kranskop, a small village about five miles from the farm. At two o'clock she was fetched, either by Kleinhans or by her father who might have business in the village. Distances between the farms were too great to allow for friendships out of school. When she was very young, she had mixed freely with the black children on the farm, though she hadn't been allowed to bring them into the house. Later she was forbidden to play with them. Andre, her only brother who was six years older, was away at boarding school for most of her childhood. At the age of twelve she too was sent to boarding school.

Her father built a small church for his labourers and a schoolroom for their children. I value education, he said. The kaffirs must learn to read and write. That way they will understand instructions better. He also valued education for his children: Andre took a degree in divinity at the University of Stellenbosch. Louise, at her own insistence, did a B.A. at the University of the Witwatersrand. In later years Johan Marais complained that from the time she breathed in the poisonous English air of Johannesburg, she had been lost to her own people.

After his father's death, Andre took over the farm. He enlarged the schoolroom, built a new church and conducted the services himself. While he tended to their spiritual needs – the labourers still lived in mud huts at the far end of the farm – his wife Marie delivered their babies, bandaged their injuries, nursed the children through illness, and taught in the schoolroom when Elias Moeng, the teacher, was too incapacitated by drink to do so. They were a happy couple, Andre and Marie, had five children, and accepted their feudal role as God-given.

'In 1925,' Sello was saying, 'we bought land from our chief Makapan for seventy pounds. Very hard here. On Frikkie's farm was good soil, much water, big fields, plenty cattle and sheep. Here we find rocks and stones, weeds and bitter water. And small place for our cattle. Every year we sell them, one, one, one, till there is nothing. We still got the cart,' he pointed to a dilapidated two-wheeled cart that held up the fence, 'but no more donkey. Only Sello is the donkey.' He laughed heartily.

'How much land have you got?' Louise asked.

'Not so much like by Baas Frikkie. In the good year we have twelve, maybe thirteen bags mealies. In the bad year only five bags. Maybe there is two morgen, Sello does not remember. Like Dikeledi say,' he smiled as Dikeledi appeared carrying five mugs of steaming tea on a battered tray, 'Sello is getting old.'

'Have some tea,' Freda said to Louise as Dikeledi brought the tray around. She raised her eyebrows, flashing an unmistakable message: don't offend our hosts.

Piqued, Louise took a mug from the tray. Freda thought she had a monopoly on good manners. Louise rested the mug on the edge of her knee as Dikeledi and Freda settled down once again to their talk. Sello held the mug between his hands, but did not drink. He was looking into the distance, his inflamed gums exposed in a wide nostalgic smile.

Louise took a tissue out of her handbag and surreptitiously rubbed the edge of her mug before she raised it to her lips.

FIVE

From behind the net curtain Joseph watched his grand-mother usher the three women into the enclosure; garden was too lush a description for the sandy area in which only the umbrella tree flourished. Desultory efforts to grow a hawthorn hedge along the fence had been made but only a few sprawling plants survived, thick in stem, sparse of leaf, with vicious stabbing thorns. Some stunted zinnias grew in a patch near the house. Their grey leaves and papery petals attested to a futile struggle against heat and drought. The fence itself was in need of repair. It was held up in one place by an old donkey cart. Perhaps after he had dug a well . . . No. Alex would be coming any day now. He had to believe that, though he did, at times, despair. One never knew with Alex. He might be detained or in hiding. He might even have left the country . . .

Joseph's heartbeats quickened, his mouth grew dry, papery. He would never get away from this village. They'd close in on him, hunt him down, he'd be put into a windowless room, tortured . . . He took a deep breath. He must not lose control. Of course Alex would come. He had promised, and Alex had never let him down.

Joseph watched Dikeledi lead the three women to the umbrella tree.

' . . . My husband, Sello,' she was saying, 'he knows English. He is coming now from the field.'

Joseph cringed. When she spoke to whites, his tall proud grandmother was transformed into a simpering

33

black nanny. It was incredible that this was the woman who had toiled and sweated over the school building, who had taken up a knobkerrie in its defence, and who had the respect of the entire village for her pride and courage. There she stood, shoulders stooped as though apologising for towering over the two white women, speaking to them in fractured English when she could tell the most wonderful tales in fluent, poetic Tswana.

'My English isn't so good either,' the fat old woman said.

It should be! You've had the education, the money, the privileges. Joseph knew these old women with their white hair tinted blue. During school holidays he had worked in a hotel in Hillbrow where a nephew of Sello's was the headwaiter. Boy, take away this meat, it's stringy; boy, there's a fly in the salad; boy, there's no salt on the table. With heavily-ringed fingers flashing gold and diamonds, they showed how many children they had, the size of their homes, the contour of their gardens. In company they bragged; in private they complained that one mother could look after ten children but that ten children could not care for one mother.

Eight rooms, an old woman once told Joseph in the lift, holding up eight fingers. And not a corner for me. Her face crumpled and Joseph thought she was going to cry. Instead, she manipulated her tongue expertly around her dentures, raised them off her gums with a clatter, then wiped away a stubborn morsel with a delicate white handkerchief.

All day these women sat in the lounge, gossiping, arguing, gesticulating, sighing. Joseph had rarely seen them read or sew or knit. Occasionally they braved the Hillbrow traffic and went into the exhaust-filled air for a short walk. They returned breathless, pale, relieved and sad to be back in their luxurious prison. An aroma of decaying flesh and rancid juices seeped through their soaps and perfumes. When they left the lounge, it reeked like a deserted chicken run.

His grandmother smelled of woodsmoke and crushed khaki weed. He remembered the musky smell that rose from her open blouse when, as a child, he had cuddled up in her lap while she told him stories.

'Do you also pray at the river?' the old woman was asking. She was fat and ugly. Joseph wondered in which hotel she lived and whether she too ordered more than she could eat, mutilated it with a blunt hotel knife, then left the mess of half-masticated food on her plate. While black children were dying of hunger . . .

Ancestors, Joseph whispered, resting his head against the cool earthen wall; purge me of this bitterness. It is poisoning my life.

He remembered the younger woman with the white, crinkle-paper face. She was the mother of Karl for whom Anna had worked for many years. Mojalefa had spent all his school holidays at their house. Joseph had envied and resented his friendship with Karl. When Mojalefa returned from his holiday wearing Karl's clothes, the other boys had sneered, white's cast-offs, but Mojalefa had not cared. Karl's my friend, he said. He understands things, he's with us. Get it straight, man, said Mafika who was always putting people straight. If he's white, he's against us. But his father's been sent to jail for twenty years, Mojalefa protested; he fought for our cause. Man, Mafika had replied, if he's white we haven't got a common cause.

Karl's mother sat quietly, listening to Dikeledi and Freda talk. Her nose was too long and her lips too thin, but her eyes were large and dark. There was suffering in

35

her face. Joseph recognised suffering, even in a white face. As she turned her face towards the house, her eyes seemed to be drowning in unshed tears. Despite himself, Joseph felt a twinge of sympathy for her. Then he turned away. To hell with her; let her suffer. What does she care for our suffering?

Perhaps Mafika was right. Where had Karl been when the police opened fire on 16 June? Not with them. The police did not shoot white students; they stuck them inside for the night. Then their parents bailed them out and sent them overseas, to safety. Mafika was no friend of his but Joseph had to admit that he understood how things were in the townships.

'Black consciousness is not enough,' Joseph argued with Mafika, echoing Alex. 'The whole economic system must be changed.'

'Communist!' Mafika responded.

'Communism isn't the only alternative to the present system. Our own culture has positive aspects. Work parties used to be organised to help other families. The land used to belong to the whole tribe . . . '

'Tribalist!' Mafika spat out with contempt.

And when he really wanted to be insulting, he called Joseph a poet, a dreamer.

And now Anna had come to complicate his life, to question him about Mojalefa. There she sat in the shade of the umbrella tree, a model of injured motherhood, heroic. There was no way Joseph could escape her. Anna would smell him out; she was a determined woman. But there was nothing he could tell her. He had not seen Mojalefa for months, not since the night of the fires. And what Alex had told him was confidential. Anna was perfectly capable of crossing the border and dragging Mojalefa home.

When Sello and Sammy came into the enclosure carrying their sacks of beans, Joseph moved away from the window. He picked up an old hessian sack and went out the back door towards the mealie plot.

SIX

The midday sun blazed down on Joseph as he walked through the dying mealies, plucking the brittle cobs from their sockets and throwing them into his sack. Later he would pull back the yellowing sheaths, tear away the silky tassles, and spread them out to dry. Runnels of sweat poured down his head into the corners of his eyes, over his cheeks, and into the sides of his mouth where he wiped them away with a scratched, roughened hand. Tomorrow he would ask Phineas, their neighbour, what they were paying for mealies this season. Phineas owned a donkey cart and dealt directly with the mill.

For many years Sipho's store had been the central depot for the villagers' harvests, but Joseph did not trust Sipho. He owned the only truck in the district, and set the maize price on a take-it-or-leave-it basis. The villagers took it; few of them had any form of transport and the mill was fifty kilometres away. Thus Sipho made a handsome profit on their harvests – how else had he acquired a brick house, a large store and a truck? – and the mill made a profit on Sipho. The only losers were his grandparents and the other farmers, who, after a season's toil, might be left with a little cash, or extended credit at Sipho's store.

Joseph waved away a fly that was circling his head. From a distance he heard Anna's voice.

'Joseph! Where are you hiding? Come out of those mealies. Joseph!'

He sighed but did not answer. Anna had always been

a battler, for the wrong causes. Alex used to describe the wild fights she had with Charlie, her husband, over his membership of the ANC. You made a family, look after it; let others do the fighting, she used to yell at him. Charlie was not ruthless like me, Alex had said. He was honest, enthusiastic but not strong enough to withstand her nagging, so he finally took to drink. But I'd trust Charlie any time, drunk or not. When the organisation was banned, he had not followed Alex and the others into exile; neither had he gone underground. He had simply joined a congress of another kind in the shebeens and beer-halls of the township.

'Joseph!' Anna called in a deep, impatient voice.

She could have been a great force in the liberation struggle, Joseph thought. Instead, she had dissipated her gifts on the respectable values of her white madams. Children must go to school and church, be obedient and clean. They must listen to their elders and not fly in the face of the System. After all, one had to get on in life, become better house boys, garden boys, garbage collectors. There was a lot of shit to be cleaned up and collected from the white suburbs.

'Joseph, I know you're in there. Come out of those mealies!'

Anna was a hypocrite. While she self-righteously condemned Charlie's drunkenness, she herself ran a shebeen in her madam's backyard. And much as she complained about him, she never let him go. A drunken husband was better than no husband, especially if he was a source of cash. She also valued the status of being a married woman; not every black mother was one. When she talked, she waved her hands about, displaying the fake diamond ring on her wedding finger. Joseph wondered how she had taken Charlie's defection. Serves her right. But Alex had been tolerant of Anna. She's brought up the children without much help from Charlie, he said. Women in our society get a raw deal. I should know, he had added.

'Joseph!'

He sighed and walked towards the compelling voice. He might as well get it over with. He would tell her what he could: he had not seen Mojalefa since 16 June and had no way of knowing where he was at present. Anna would also want to know about her other children, if she did not know already. There was no joy in store for her today.

She was standing at the edge of the mealie plot. Her head was bound in a green floral doek which matched the loose-fitting dress that draped her full figure. With her head held high and her shoulders back, she looked taller than she was. Her face was unwrinkled, ageless. She could have been thirty or sixty; Africa is kind to its own. MaNthatisi might have looked like this as she stood on the fastness of Kooaneng, or when she led her hordes in the raids that had devastated the southern highveld. Right now it was Joseph who was about to be devastated, and he did not relish the prospect. This is no MaNthatisi, he had to remind himself. This is Anna, domestic servant, shebeen queen, and over-ambitious mother of his best friend Mojalefa.

'So, Joseph, why do you hide from me? What bad news are you concealing?' Anna launched into the attack immediately. 'Or are you hiding your face in shame after the sorrows you have caused your mother?'

'Neither, Mmamogolo,' Joseph answered, angry. She ought not to have brought his mother into this. 'I have been living with my grandparents for the last eight months. What news can I have? I can only tell you that the price Sipho has fixed for the mealies is too low.'

'Cheeky boy. For all the polite titles you give me and that soft voice you speak with, I can see into your dark soul. It is blacker than your face. You always were a deep one. Mmamogolo, he calls me. I am not older than your own mother so you must call me Mmane. But let that pass. When did you last see Mojalefa and where is he now? He would not go anywhere without telling you. You and Mojo are like this.' She crossed her fingers.

'The last time I saw Mojalefa was on the night of 16 June,' Joseph said, looking directly into Anna's eyes.

'I believe you. But you know more. I have heard rumours of strange cars that come into the village at night.'

'Those who tell you such tales have bitten your ear,' Joseph replied, slipping into the speech patterns of his grandmother. 'You know that Mojalefa is in my chest. He is my best friend. For that reason I too would like news of him.'

Anna looked at him doubtfully.

'Mmane Anna,' Joseph pressed on, 'it is I who should be asking you questions. You are in the city. In the village there are no newspapers and few radios. All I hear is rumours, and the only news I have read is from the piece of newspaper Sipho wraps our groceries in. And then I always get the stock exchange page. How are things in the townships?'

'In the townships there is weeping and sorrow,' Anna said, relenting. 'What else can there be when you and your friends burn and destroy and wake up a hatred that's been sleeping for so long? I know the words widow and orphan. But what do you call a mother who has lost her child? Tell me, you made me such a one.'

'Children have died before this trouble, from hunger and poverty. That is what we are trying to change,' Joseph said. 'But tell me more. Are the schools open? Do the hippos still come every day? With the dogs? Did people stay away from work?'

Anna looked at him, tight-lipped. 'Do you mock me, Joseph, or is it possible you do not know?'

'I do not mock you, Mmane Anna. I do not know what goes on in the outside world. I hear only rumours. This village is worse than any jail. Its walls go up the sky.'

'Mothers are still queuing outside the mortuary,' Anna said softly. 'Children are roaming the streets. Soweto is a graveyard of burnt-out cars and burnt-out buildings. The police and their dogs are there every day. No one goes out after dark. And when the sun goes down and it becomes quiet, you can hear weeping from the houses. They say hundreds died, thousands are still in hospital. We do not know how many there are in prison. It was quiet for a little while, then in August it began again. Don't go to work, your school friends are shouting. Stay at home. And starve? The young ones don't understand. And every day, every day, the ones who are not in jail or in hospital are going away for training.' Anna's voice faltered.

'What do you want?' She raised her voice suddenly. 'What are you trying to do? Look how hard we work to keep you at school. The books, the fees, the uniforms. Big boys in Standard Three who should be working. Your lives are too easy. Your mothers and fathers wake at four to do the whites' washing, to work in their factories. And you stay at home to burn and destroy. When I started school, my mother sewed me a dress from washed-out flour bags, a Blue Ribbon dress. And in winter my feet cracked from the cold because I did not have shoes. I cried when my mother took me out of school in Standard Six. I wanted to learn more. But I had to go and work and send my brothers and sisters to school.'

Joseph watched a toktokkie lumber across the sandy

soil towards the mealie patch. He was tired of flour-bag dresses, cracked feet, frustrated educational aspirations. These Annas and Ellens would never understand, never see beyond their own lives.

' . . . and that Alex is behind all this, I know,' Anna was saying. 'He is using the young ones for his own purposes. I'll kill him with my own two hands when I see him. He was also the devil who tempted Charlie into bad ways. If not for him, Charlie would never have joined the ANC and turned to drink.'

Joseph did not correct her elliptical conclusion. Perhaps she really did not understand Charlie's frustrations nor her own part in his tragedy.

'You must know where Mojalefa is,' she said, quietly now. 'Tell me. It may not be too late.'

Joseph hesitated, then said, 'Mmane, I do not know where Mojalefa is.'

To his surprise, Anna collapsed in a heap on the ground, buried her face in her hands and began to weep and rock herself back and forth.

'Ai, ai, ai, all is lost! He has gone for training. He will be killed. He will return to kill his own brothers. His brothers . . . '

She stopped crying. 'That is something you must know. How are his brothers? Are Willie, Abram and Peter going to school? I have not yet had time to speak properly to your grandmother about them.'

Joseph looked away. She repeated her question as she got up from the ground, dusting her dress and wiping her nose with a crumpled tissue.

'They are, well,' he said.

'Speak with a full mouth, man!' she cried. 'Can you not reply to a simple question? They are well, he says, turning his eyes from my bleeding heart. Speak out, speak out!'

43

'Willie and Abram have not been to school since it opened, two months ago,' Joseph said angrily. 'Willie is working on de Wet's farm, helping to bring in the mealies, and Abram helps Sipho take the mealies to the mill. Peter is still at school.'

Anna was silent for a while. She stared out beyond the mealies toward the river where the Zionists were still singing. She clenched and unclenched her fists rapidly.

'I do not understand why the Ancestors are heaping such sorrows on my head,' she said finally. 'I just wanted my children to have enough education to keep them from the mealie fields of the Boers and from the kitchens of the white madams. All is for nothing. I wait only to hear that Willie and Abram have joined their brother on the other side.' She turned to go. Joseph felt a pang of regret; her sorrow was real.

'Mmane Anna,' he said, putting his hand lightly on her shoulder.

She shook it off, her eyes blazing.

'You destroyers, you! If you had ever built anything, you would not be in such a fever to destroy.'

'They never gave us a chance to build,' he said. 'They made us into destroyers.'

But Anna was no longer listening. With her head held higher than before, she walked around the front of the house and disappeared from view.

SEVEN

Joseph lay down among the mealie plants, his head on his forearm. He had not meant to hurt Anna, but while he respected his grandmother's friends, he felt threatened by his mother's. They were always shouting, ordering you about, weeping, turning your insides to pap. If you listened to them, you would never be free. They had cast aside the old traditions and tried to ape the whites. How ridiculous they looked in their tight dresses and high-heeled shoes which made their bums bounce about like jellies. They wore wigs to hide their hair, pencilled their eyes, lightened their skins and drew ugly red lips over their mouths. In a shop window near Park Station, he once counted twenty-three different brands of skin lightener. Anna, of course, was not a fancy lady but all she ever cared about was her own family, and to hell with everyone else's.

Oh Mojalefa, where are you? Joseph turned over onto his back and looked up at the pale hot sky. He had always known where Mojalefa was. They had grown up within calling distance of one another in the homes of their maternal grandmothers. They started school together and sat on the floor of the dark, ceilingless classroom with boys and girls of different ages. There were only five double desks, and these were occupied by the children of the school committee. When he told Dikeledi, she marched into the classroom the following morning, and ignoring the astounded teacher, gently moved the children out of the desks. She picked out ten children at random – Joseph was not among them – then said to the teacher: the school was built for all the children. Share everything well between them.

Joseph had never again complained about school. The teacher, a thin bespectacled, buck-toothed woman who claimed kinship to Chief Makapan, had been mortified by Dikeledi's behaviour, and took it out on Joseph. Barely a day passed when she did not punish him on one pretext or another. At first he felt humiliated; later he gave her grounds for her victimisation. In all his escapades, Mojalefa had been his faithful henchman.

At the age of twelve, they ran away from home. Joseph stole a rand from Sello's old snuff box, and Mojalefa took food from his grandmother's kitchen. They walked fifty kilometres to town, bought a bag of oranges and set up as fruit vendors at the bus station. Vusumi, an older boy who sold newspapers, rented them a corner of his township shack. But just as the citrus business was taking off, Anna and Alex swooped down on them. Anna laid into Mojalefa with all the might of betrayed motherhood. Alex, on the hand, started a dialogue with Joseph which, with long breaks, continued to the present day. Joseph had not recognised Alex; he had been a baby when Alex left the first time. His grandparents spoke of Alex as Ellen's husband, and he wondered if this made him his father.

He and Mojalefa had been taken back to the village where Dikeledi, with tears and a flat hand, chastised him. She and Ramasela then handed over responsibility for them to their daughters in Johannesburg. Mojalefa went to live with his mother's aunt in Soweto, not far from where Joseph was to live with his mother and Alex. That was the time Malome Benedict had given Joseph the penknife, together with his prophecy of fire and destruction.

Joseph got off the ground, brushed the ants from his

sweating limbs, and continued gathering in the mealies. Just thinking about that period made his stomach knot up; he had never been so miserable. He missed his grand-mother, his friends, the open fields; he even missed the school where he had received his daily portion of unjust treatment.

The boys called him plaas skapie, country bumpkin, the girls sniggered at his clothes. He's growing too fast, his mother complained; it's a waste to buy him a school uniform. Had it not been for Alex – and Zandile – he would have run back to the village. Eventually he made friends among the students who belonged to the school's literary society. Once a year they produced a cyclostyled magazine called *New Outlook*. The previous year Joseph's poem 'Dawn Raid' had appeared in it. He had signed it *Senkatana*. When the news leaked out that he was Senkatana, he was subjected to more baiting and teasing.

'They're jealous,' Zandile consoled him. Then, like a butterfly brushing his cheek, she had kissed him. 'The poem is wonderful. You speak for all of us.'

That's what the police thought as well. 'We want the tall one, the one with the penknife who calls himself Senka-tana,' they had told Zandile when they took her in on the night of the fires. 'Tell us where he is and you'll go free.'

Later Alex had brought him to Zandile. Her face was swollen, a front tooth was missing, and both her eyes were black and puffy. Alex had left them alone for only a few minutes.

'She must leave right away,' Alex had said. 'They know she's your friend and they'll use her to get you.'

Joseph threw down his bag of mealies and sat down, his face in his hands. Zandile, Zandile, there's so much I left unsaid. His chest contracted painfully. Only tears could relieve it but he had forbidden himself to cry, or to think of Zandile. But he could not control his dreams. Zandile's image seemed indelibly etched on his eyelids, and when he closed his eyes, she was there: tall, straight, with rounded limbs and soft brown eyes . . . If Alex did not come soon, he would go to that house in the village or make his own way across the border. Perhaps Alex was testing him . . . He breathed deeply, and the pain in his chest subsided. Alex would never let him down. He must discipline himself and wait.

It had taken him some time to piece together Alex's place in his life. Ellen's house in Soweto was small, its walls thin. But even through the deepest dungeons he would have heard his mother's shrill voice blaming Alex for all the misfortunes in her life. They had married in 1955. Even then, it seemed, Alex had been totally involved in politics. He was away a great deal and Ellen had been left to fend for herself. Joseph was born two years after their marriage.

'A woman cannot live alone,' she used to taunt Alex with Joseph's paternity. 'He's my son all right, never mind his father. All you men know is to . . . '

Joseph winced when he thought of Ellen's vocabulary. His grandparents never swore. Were they really Ellen's parents? Was he really Ellen's son? Biological father or not, Alex, in the years they spent together, had given him more love and direction than anyone else in his life except Dikeledi. But with Ellen he wanted no kinship. In response to her taunts, Alex would gaze at Joseph, studying his face for a trace of himself. He found none: only Ellen's features were there, duplicated faithfully on Joseph's face.

'Melt away the likeness!' Joseph ordered the blazing sun

which was now directly above his head. 'I am no son of hers.'

He had hardly known Ellen in his childhood. She had brought him to his grandparents when he was two, soon after Alex left. She came to the village twice a year, at Easter and at Christmas, wept all over him, smothered him in kisses, then seemed to forget all about him in the time between. He always held his breath as she embraced him, overcome by the smell of sweat and scent.

Joseph had grown close to Alex, despite his absences. Even when home, Alex had left at dawn and returned after dark. In this he was no different from other township fathers, except that most children knew where their fathers worked. Joseph never asked; he intuitively respected Alex's need for privacy. As their relationship developed and deepened, Alex spoke more openly about his political commitment.

'My freedom depends on your silence,' Alex had told him.

'I'll die before I talk,' was his fervent reply.

'Spoken like Senkatana,' Alex laughed.

Dikeledi had given Joseph an insight into his traditional culture; Alex gave him perspective on the modern world.

Ellen resented their closeness. 'He may not even be your son,' she would say.

Once, when her taunts had become unbearable, Alex had slapped her. The rest of the night rang with sobs, apologies, more taunts, shouts, then silence, followed by the groaning of bedsprings. Joseph had tossed about restlessly in his narrow bed, covered his ears, pulled the blankets over his head, but nothing had shut out the creak of the bedsprings.

'Why did you marry her?' Joseph asked Alex the next morning.

'Because I loved her. We went through high school together and I was her first lover. We only grew apart when I went to university. People like me,' he said, 'should not love, marry or have children. I carry a heavy load of guilt about Ellen. After I went away, when you were just two years old, she led a wild life. When I returned, I wanted to rescue her from it.' He laughed ruefully. 'These days Ellen can hardly wait to be abandoned again.'

Alex left a second time when Joseph was fourteen.

'I'll be back,' he promised Joseph, 'but I cannot say when. Look after Ellen, share my burden. And take care of Sammy.'

'Just like the last time!' Ellen raged. 'That vokenbastard looks at me with full eyes like he wants to piss and says look after yourself and he's gone. Never mind one child I brought up with my hard work behind a till in Haroun's stinking shop in Vietas with him watching every penny I put into it. Now he goes and leaves me with this one.'

She gestured angrily towards Sammy, a fifteen-month-old infant with a runny nose and rheumy eyes.

'And where's he gone?' Ellen shouted. 'Don't ask me. To be a soldier, to change the system, who knows what or where. He never tells me anything. The less you know the less you'll tell them, he says. I'll go straight to the Office if he comes back. Come fetch him, I'll say. Send your kwela-kwelas and your blackjacks. Torture him, throw him out the window, give him one of your special showers. If I get hold of him I'll cut off his blerry prick and stuff it down his throat!'

Joseph wrote to his grandmother that Alex had left and that Ellen couldn't look after Sammy. Within a week Dikeledi arrived in Soweto. Two years had passed since Joseph had seen her and he was not ashamed of the tears that flowed down his face when she embraced him, enveloping him in the smell of khaki weed and woodsmoke.

'You did not come to visit us,' she reproached him.

'In the holidays I work in the hotel to get money for school and books,' he told her.

'Help your mother,' Dikeledi had said when he took her and Sammy to the station a few days later. 'She's had a hard life. Don't mind her words; they cannot harm you. She's got a good heart.'

Her good heart was not evident to Joseph. She seemed to begrudge every mouthful of food he ate.

'The appetite of Kgodumodumo,' she complained. 'And the school fees, the books, the clothes . . .'

She never talked to Joseph; she gave him orders. Buy bread, fetch mealie meal, pay the rent, light the stove, clean the kitchen. And after a night of heavy drinking in the kitchen-dining room which had been converted into a shebeen within a week of Alex's departure, there was plenty to clean up: spilled beer, cigarette ends, empty cans and bottles, and often the vomit of a surfeited customer who had not made it to the backyard.

Every evening Joseph prepared a small meal for himself; Ellen ate later with her customers. Then he took his books into his tiny room and shut the door against the stream of strangers who came knocking at all hours, demanding drink and entertainment. A friend – Ellen had a collection of useful 'friends' – installed a record player in the kitchen, and loud music blared into the early hours of the morning, punctuated by even louder voices, laughter and an occasional fight.

Joseph woke at dawn, lit the stove, cooked himself a thin porridge, then cleaned up the kitchen. Occasionally he'd find a drunk sprawled over a table or lying in a pool of vomit or urine. If Joseph rushed off to school without doing his chores, Ellen was furious.

'I break my back to keep you fed and clothed and you don't do anything for your keep!' she shouted.

Joseph wasn't surprised that her back was broken. The bedsprings were strained to breaking point every night. Yet she seemed to need him in some mysterious way. She used him as a buffer against people like Lucky, for example. Lucky was Ellen's 'protector'. He arrived at about eleven every morning in his green Kombi and took her into town to buy supplies for the evening. He was said to 'know the law'. He certainly knew whom to bribe. As a result their house was rarely raided, and when it was, they had ample warning. Lucky ran a fleet of taxis and supervised a chain of shebeens in the township. He was much older than Ellen and she treated him with fear or respect, Joseph was not certain which.

Joseph had never seen Lucky raise a hand to Ellen, nor had he heard him shout. When he was angry, he would sit at one of the small tables that cluttered up the kitchen, drum his fingers monotonously on it, and speak in a cool voice, his eyes half closed. He reminded Joseph of Sydney Greenstreet whom he had once seen in a movie. Perhaps Lucky had seen the same film. His head was completely shaven and he had a glistening roll of fat above his neck. Joseph found that even more revolting than the huge belly that strained against the buttons of his shirt.

Ellen always nudged Joseph into the room when Lucky arrived, playing the role of affectionate mother. Very unconvincingly, Joseph thought, though it seemed to take Lucky in. I need an educated man around, Lucky told him. If you leave school, you can be my personal assistant. I'll teach you everything I know about the business. Joseph declined the offer politely, much to Ellen's chagrin.

When Alex returned, four years later, he did not go to Ellen's house. One day a stranger approached Joseph in the school grounds during the lunch break.

'From Alex to Senkatana,' the man had said, giving the password which Alex, with a wry smile, had arranged to use.

Later that evening Joseph and Alex had met behind Motana's store. Alex was thinner than Joseph remembered. His hair was bushier, greyer, and he was wearing gold-rimmed spectacles. Joseph barely recognised him. But when Alex put his hand on Joseph's shoulder and greeted him in his deep warm voice, all the affection whch Joseph had felt for him came rushing back.

'You've grown so tall,' Alex said. 'I left a boy of fourteen and I find a man of eighteen.'

'It's been so long.' Joseph's voice wavered.

'There's much to talk about, many years to catch up on.'

They sat down on two paraffin tins behind Motana's store and Joseph filled him in on the missing years. There was little concerning Ellen's life, however, that had not reached Alex in the furthest corners of Africa and beyond.

'It is better that Ellen and I should not live together,' Alex had said. 'It can only cause us pain.'

Joseph, however, met him regularly in different parts of Soweto. Alex and Ellen did not meet again until the night of the fires.

EIGHT

The heat, the steady drone of conversation which switched from magic and medicine to folk stories, and the emotional toll from her visit to Tony that morning, made Louise doze off. She was woken by a drop of sweat trickling down her temple. The sun was now directly above them and the umbrella tree had drawn in its shade, leaving her on its periphery.

'I not have time to tell my children the stories,' Dikeledi was saying. 'Too much work and troubles. But with Joseph, son of my daughter Ellen, with him I sit in the night when the cattle are in the kraal and the moon is coming up, and tell him plenty plenty stories. He likes the story of Kgodumodumo who eats up the people and Senkatana who makes them free. Also the story why the dassie not got a tail.'

'Tell me why it hasn't got a tail,' Freda said.

'It is raining on that day the Lord gives tails to the animals. The dassie not want to be wet. Go fetch me a tail, he tell to the rabbit. But the rabbit she forget, so the dassie not got a tail. If you want a tail, you must get wet, I say to Joseph. He laugh and laugh but he remember.'

'I'd like to meet Joseph,' Freda said.

'He is by the mealies. Here is Anna. Child of my friend, have you seen Joseph?'

'He is in the field,' Anna replied, wiping away the traces of her tears with a tissue. 'He says he does not know where is Mojalefa. But I know. He is where all the other boys are, where all the others will go.' She turned to Louise. 'When the madam is ready we can go home. Willie and Abram are not in the village, Peter is with my mother. There is nothing here for me. Joseph has told me everything,' she said to Dikeledi who sighed, stretched out her hands helplessly, then dropped them into her lap.

'Children.' Freda sighed in unison with Dikeledi. 'We mothers have nothing but sorrow from the day they are born. But we should also be proud of them. They are braver than their fathers. They will make a new world.'

Louise looked angrily at Freda. There was something obscene about the way Freda clung to her illusions.

'You don't build new worlds in captivity, in exile or with violence,' Louise said bitterly. 'Besides, who wants to live in a new world nourished by the blood of our children?'

Freda glared at her sharply but did not reply. She's thinking that blood is thicker than water, Louise guessed, and that even the best Afrikaners – Freda was very fond of Louise – could never really transcend their background and upbringing: Calvinist, reactionary, racist.

Perhaps it was true; perhaps she would one day speak like her father. She remembered the interminable arguments they'd had in the old farmhouse kitchen while her mother stood over the stove, cooking, baking, pickling, preserving.

'The persecuted,' Louise had said of their Huguenot ancestors, 'eventually became the persecutors.'

'We were never persecutors,' Johan Marais had said vehemently. Though proud of his Huguenot descent, his family had intermarried with Dutch and German settlers and he considered himself a ware, a true Afrikaner. Only the name Marais lingered as a reminder of his origins. 'We fled from British tyranny, we always valued freedom.'

'For yourselves. What of your Hottentot slaves? When your ancestors (and yours, he interpolated) went on the Great Trek, there were more slaves and servants in their entourage than trekkers.'

'They came willingly,' he said.

'And what of the black people you displaced as you went along?'

'We came to an empty land,' he replied.

'An empty land! That's what all colonialists say. Indigenous people are like the rocks and the hills and the beasts of the field to them. You came to a land devastated by Zulu and Ndebele warlords,' she conceded, 'but what of the ordinary people, the black farmers and pasturalists? The land was theirs. You either drove them away or enslaved them.'

'Pasturalists, farmers,' Johan Marais said with infinite contempt. 'Shaka, Mzilikazi and the other black butchers killed more of their own people than we ever did in all the wars we fought against them. The land is ours by conquest. We fought to survive, they killed for power.'

'Survival!' By this stage Louise was unable to sustain an unemotional argument. 'That's the dirtiest word in the language. In the name of survival the worst crimes are committed.'

No. It was unlikely that she would ever speak like her father. Nor, for that matter, would she ever think like Tony.

'I don't feel at ease with your comrades,' she had told Tony after she had been to several meetings with him. 'They are arrogant and rigid. They revile Hitler and revere Stalin, both of them fascists as far as I'm concerned. They patronise the blacks who ask questions and scoff at the whites who express doubts.'

Naive, unpoliticised, bourgeois, Tony had labelled her.

In those years it had seemed to Louise that the Party members were playing at revolution. The persecution, harassment, torture and incarceration to which they were later subjected gave to their earlier activities a retrospective dignity and meaning which Louise was not sure they deserved. But it had also separated the dilettantes from the dedicated and Louise had a fractured admiration for their courage.

She had first met Tony when he addressed a meeting on the lawn outside the university library. He had been introduced as Tony Buchman, final year architecture student from the University of Cape Town. She stopped to listen but did not hear much of what he said. Her eyes lingered over his cheekbones and the high forehead which was wrinkled with earnestness. His hazel eyes – so much like Freda's – had darkened with anger as he described the iniquities of the Group Areas Act. Then he caught her eye and held it throughout his talk. When she moved into the shade of the prunus tree which was in full bloom, his eyes followed her. She had not known whether she was breathless from the smell of the blossoms or from the intensity of his gaze. After the meeting he came straight towards her, took her by the arm and said, 'Let's have coffee.'

She had never met anyone like Tony. He was intense, exuberant, sensitive, angry; she never knew in which direction his volatile moods would blow him. She had been in love before, first with Johan, an engineering student from a staid anglicised Afrikaner family, then with Clifford, her English tutor. Clifford had worked over her heavy Platteland accent so thoroughly, that her carefully enunciated English drew fire from Tony.

'Oh, those O's!' He clutched his head in mock horror. 'Give me a good old chatas accent any time.'

'Does your political commitment licence you to use racist terminology?' she had asked.

'Don't be a prig,' he said. 'We're all racists in this crazy country. To work it out of our system, we first have to recognise that, then reject it. I wonder what nasty little prejudices your parents implanted in you?'

He had smiled sceptically when she said, 'I've worked through mine.'

She and Tony were mismatched from the start. He was Jewish, intellectual, passionate and politically committed. He had an urban, liberal background and a scientific training. She was Afrikaans, rural, compassionate, with a distrust of politics and with a strong sense of justice. She had majored in English literature and wrote poetry secretly. But she and Tony were so much in love that they ignored their differences. They could not be near one another without touching or losing themselves in each other's eyes.

Years later, during a prison visit, they'd had a rare personal discussion. Tony dissected their marriage coldly, clinically.

'It was a disaster,' he concluded. 'You should have married that sensitive English tutor of yours – aesthetic, spiritual, all soul.'

'And you?'

'People like me shouldn't marry at all,' he had said.

A rare feeling of pity for him washed over her.

'You were my great love,' she said softly.

He looked at her with an incredulous expression on his face then laughed, loudly, with something of his old exuberance.

'Louise, you are a compulsive non-negator. Think of those miserable years! Besides, one does not marry one's great love, that's what keeps it great.'

You should know, she wanted to say; you did not marry yours. But she smiled and did not reply. Prison hadn't blunted Tony's talent for inflicting pain. He read the look on her face and shrugged.

'To survive,' he said grimly, 'one must have no regrets.'

'To survive,' she answered, turning her face away from him, 'one must not negate.'

After he graduated, Tony had taken a job with a firm of architects in Johannesburg. Louise had enrolled at Teachers' Training College. They moved into a tiny bachelor flat near the university and when she fell pregnant towards the end of her course, they had married. Without her parents' blessings.

'Jew! Communist! Seducer!' her father had called Tony during their disastrous visit to the farm.

'Irrefutable facts.' Tony had acknowledged the epithets with seeming nonchalance, but he turned very pale.

Her mother, as usual, stood quietly in the background, her eyes cast down, while her brother Andre, wearing his Sunday mien, looked grieved.

Louise never went home again, not even after her parents died. She was later reconciled with Andre, who, despite the will, had insisted on giving her a small share of the estate. Karl and Freddie had grown up without knowing their cousins. She had cried all the way home after that visit. I have no family now but you, she had said to Tony. Join the Party, he'd said, and you'll have extended family for life.

' . . . for life,' Freda was saying to Dikeledi in a subdued voice. 'But we know better, my son and I. Soon he will be liberated, together with all the other oppressed people.'

Louise pretended not to hear. If Freda insisted on living

in a world of fantasy, that was her affair. She looked at Sello whose chin had dropped onto his chest. He snored loudly, then woke suddenly, looking sheepish.

'Sello is old. Never before did he sleep in the day,' he said. 'Now he sleeps, with plenty dreams. Running, shooting, dust from the cattle . . . ' He coughed. 'Too much dust.'

'You said you'd tell me where you learned English,' Louise reminded him.

'Many years we try to make a farm from this bitter land,' he said, 'but the children are born thin and sick and to get food I must go to town for work. I work for many years for Mrs Weinstein in Doornfontein. Flat boy. The master is always sick and just Mrs Weinstein and Sello looks after the flats. Every day four o'clock when I am finished the cleaning, I have the shower, and go to Mrs Weinstein's kitchen. She gives me food and teaches me the English. Every day, every day for fourteen years. I am learning very good, I like so much the books. Even when I am going back home, she send me food and newspapers and sometimes a dress for Dikeledi. Two years now she is dead. She was our mother. It is nearly time for all the old people to go to their Ancestors. But no hurry.' He laughed.

'And who worked on the farm when you were in town?' Louise asked.

'Dikeledi. And Pitso and Benedict, before the war. But there is not enough to eat from the field. If you want to eat, you must go to the town.'

'I understand,' Freda said. 'When we were small children in Russia, my father didn't have work, so he went to Africa, to look for gold. He didn't find any, and it took seven years before he could save enough money to bring us to Africa. My mother had a hard time in the old country.

She had five children to feed. She got up at four o'clock every morning to bake yeast buns and bread for a bakery. My father sent a little money, but it wasn't enough. My oldest brother was apprenticed to a tailor when he was twelve, and he made his own suit for his barmitzvah, his thirteenth birthday,' she explained.

Dikeledi clucked sympathetically but looked puzzled. Freda laughed.

'You're thinking how can white people be so poor? You should have seen the ghettoes and the villages where the Jews lived in Eastern Europe. Some of them looked even worse than Alexandra township. It was a little easier in the bigger towns but in the far-off villages we were cut off from everything. Like here,' she said.

'Everyone was white?' Dikeledi looked incredulous.

'We were the blacks of Europe,' Freda said, 'like you are the Jews of Africa. We couldn't own land, we had to live apart from everyone else, we were not allowed, until after the Revolution, to go to universities though every Jewish child was taught to read and write and study the Bible. We could not get proper jobs and were not allowed into some towns in Russia without special permission. On top of this, when the local priest thought we were getting too fat and happy, he told his people that the Jews had killed their Lord and they fell upon us and murdered us. Pogroms, they were called. You've had a few of them yourselves.'

Dikeledi nodded, Sello sighed. Anna, with bent head and arms hanging loosely at her sides, sat apart from them in silence.

Freda has a good face, Louise thought, watching her animated movements as she talked. Her large hazel eyes (so like Tony's) under dark arched eyebrows, contrasted dramatically with her white hair. She had a straight nose, a friendly smile, good teeth and fewer wrinkles than Louise. Only her throat showed the ravages of time. What gave her face its specialness, however, was the tremendous vitality that drew all the features together.

' . . . my grandmother was a wonderful woman,' Freda said. 'It was from her that I learned all my songs and all those remedies . . . '

She was back on her favourite subject – medicine. Freda had a morbid fear of illness. The thought of dying a protracted death was one of the few fears Freda admitted to.

'I want to die at ninety,' she used to say, 'shot by a jealous lover.'

This was not such an improbable death. Louise had never imagined that someone of Freda's age and girth could still be attractive to men. Yet she was. In the few months that Freda had been living with her, Louise had met a series of 'old friends', all of whom treated Freda with great affection and respect. There was that Italian painter who had been a prisoner of war in South Africa during World War II and whom Freda had befriended when he returned as an immigrant after the war; the stamp dealer who claimed a distant kinship with her father; the retired lawyer who had been an adviser to the union; the trade unionist who, Freda used to say, had never sold out, and a few others. Why don't you marry, Louise had asked her. Once is enough, Freda had replied. Marriage turns the kindest man into a tyrant.

Freda had divorced her husband two months after Tony's barmitzvah, the last rite of passage she felt she owed her son in a family context. Tony often spoke of the fierce fights that had raged about him during his childhood.

'Exploiter!' Freda would yell at her husband Gershon, a clothing manufacturer.

'Betrayer!' he retaliated. 'Your infidelities I can forgive, but to bring out my workers on strike – there's a limit to disloyalty.'

He blamed Freda for Tony's political involvement and subsequent imprisonment. They never saw one another when he flew in from Cape Town to visit Tony in jail. Louise fetched him at the airport and drove him to Pretoria. Father and son had little to say to one another and Louise filled in the awkward silences. Gershon was a quiet, reserved man, no one's picture of a wicked capitalist exploiter. He was active in communal life and gave generously to charity.

'Charity!' Freda scoffed. 'A sop to his conscience, a prop for a corrupt system.'

She had never taken alimony from him. Before Freda had moved in with Louise, Gershon used to sleep over at the house. He had even less contact with his grand-children than he had with his son. His only way of showing love was to send Louise a generous cheque from time to time. Louise accepted it gratefully but with misgivings; Freda and Tony would have spurned it. She had liberated herself without difficulty from her own parents' values; Freda's and Tony's were more difficult to slough off. But she liked Gershon too much to hurt him.

Louise picked up a dry twig from under her chair and drew a pattern in the dust. She was tired of Freda's stories about hunger and cold, persecution and poverty, and she found her songs depressing. They were all about abandoned wives and faithless lovers, orphaned children, hammers and workers. Louise had never heard a cheerful Yiddish song. Just as all French songs sounded like love songs to her, so all Yiddish songs, particularly the love songs, sounded like dirges. But that was as it should be; there could be no happy love songs.

'Hau! Wragitg! Shame!' Dikeledi and Sello exclaimed as Freda described her childhood in a Lithuanian village. Anna said nothing. She remained on the edge of the circle, wrapped in her private grief.

'Anyone who has seen such things, anyone who has suffered,' Freda said, 'must feel for the suffering of others. And that makes us brothers and sisters in humanity. We can all live together in peace – but only after our oppressors have been overthrown.'

It was precisely this naivety, this childlike faith in human nature, which kept Freda bouyant and hopeful, Louise thought. Unlike Tony, Freda did not need to bolster a basically cynical view of life with isms as he did. When Freda spoke of revolution, she did not envisage bombs, blood or death. For her, revolution meant sitting under an umbrella tree, making human contact.

'So, where's this Joseph of yours?' Freda said to Dikeledi. 'I'd like to meet him before we leave.'

Dikeledi got up and gently roused Sammy who had fallen asleep under the tree. She spoke to him softly, in Tswana. He stood up, stretched, gave a few rasping coughs, then moved off in the direction of the mealie field.

NINE

Joseph pulled the bag of mealies along the ground towards the kitchen. Enough mealie picking for the day. When it was cooler, after the visitors left, he would fetch the pick from Malome Benedict's hut and begin working on the well. He wiped the dust off his watch. Five to twelve. The symbolic hour, Alex had called it when he came to visit Joseph the first time.

'The whites are in a panic,' he had told Joseph. 'They've suddenly realised that time is running out. Everybody's rushing around shouting, 'Five to twelve! Five to twelve! Give rights, votes, schools. Write to the editor, hold protest meetings, DO something!' But the trouble with them is that they can't tell time. It's five past twelve, not five to twelve. And the time for giving has passed. It is time for taking. You should see the queues outside the foreign embassies. Houses are going for a song, rifle clubs are flourishing and money is pouring out of the country into Swiss banks. What do liberals DO when a revolution begins? They don't know. But the Nats do: send in the tanks and mow them down.'

Alex had taken his watch off and put it on Joseph. 'Keep it,' he said. 'Not that time means anything in this godforsaken hole, but it might be useful later. I'll be back,' he had promised. Joseph's anxiety lessened. He could depend on Alex; he had never let him down.

It was cool and dark inside the house. The skinny ginger cat which had given birth to three dead kittens the

65

previous day, came out of her bloodied rags and rubbed herself against his legs. Her belly hung low, her teats were cracked and dry. She mewed pathetically. Joseph went out to the kitchen and brought back a lidful of milk. Then he lay down on the bed, listening to the steady drone of voices from under the umbrella tree and to the roof tick as it expanded in the heat.

He had expanded in the warmth of Alex's companionship. Joseph thought of the many times they had met in the dark alley behind Motana's general store. The front of the shop was brightly lit. That was where the young men of the neighbourhood congregated. They sat around on the concrete steps, in their Pringle sweaters and Florsheim shoes, with no place to go and nothing to do. They barely noticed as he and Alex walked to the back of the shop, sat down on the rusting paraffin tins, and Alex told Joseph about his life.

He had grown up in a shanty town made from the white man's rubbish: cardboard, oil drums, corrugated iron and sacking. Emasakeni, they were called, hessian sheds. There were no drains or toilets, only pits with buckets. Twenty families shared two taps, for which there were always queues.

'My father begged and borrowed and even stole to send us four children to school,' Alex told Joseph. 'My mother left at five in the morning to do washing in the white suburbs. Police raids for permits, passes, taxes and beer brewing were daily occurrences, and we children ran through the muddy alleys of our shanty-town shouting, Ikwela-kwela – things are bad – when the police vans appeared. Things haven't changed much, have they? Even the township diet has remained the same: pap and coffee for breakfast, vetkoek for lunch, stamp mealies with beans for supper. We had meat and vegetables only on Sunday.'

His family had lived in one room and slept on potato bags stuffed with grass and pillows filled with chicken feathers. 'My head still prickles when I think of it,' he said.

Alex had not talked much about his school days or about his university studies. All he said was, 'We got a better education as Natives than you did as Bantus.' He always managed to laugh, even in his most bitter moments. Joseph envied him that gift.

He tossed about restlessly on his bed. He was hot and sweaty and longed to walk down to the river and let the cool sluggish waters flow over him. But the Zionists were spread out along the river bank in their flowing white robes, singing, dancing, praying. Joseph resented them. They distracted the people from their real problems, promising them a better life in a black heaven presided over by their Ancestors. Above their hallelujahs and ululations, he could hear the persistent voice of the old white woman, urging his grandparents to change their lives.

'It's no good waiting for the System to do anything; it suits them that the land doesn't yield enough for a family to live on. That's the way it gets cheap labour to the cities. You must organise. Form a committee, raise money between all of you and buy a tractor. One of your young men can learn to use it. You can plough communally, buy your seed cheaper and market your mealies together. You need to make your voices heard. Like a trade unionist once said to a group of apathetic workers: 'Don't let them shit on your head – open your mouths!'

'Madam,' there was an impatient note in Anna's voice. 'My people are too old and too tired to make committees.

And the young ones don't come back from the cities. From where will we get the money for a tractor? And who will drive it? All the young men are gone. And the small ones will also go.'

Good for her. The years of domestic servitude had not entirely extinguished Anna's spirit. But Joseph was reluctantly impressed with the old woman's ideas.

'What on earth do you expect them to do?' Karl's mother sounded exasperated.

'Sello says his friend the Captain collects taxes from the people to give to the chief. Well, let the chief work for it. He does nothing but fleece you and buy himself new cars. Let the Captain and Sello go to him and say – no help for us, no taxes for you. My son could've given you good advice,' she added. 'He knows about landless black people. Fourteen years he's been in prison. He watched his children grow up in photographs. But things will change, Sello, you'll see.'

'Sello is too old. Maybe my grandchildren will see.'

'Don't say that!' the old woman replied. 'You'll see it yourself.'

'We should think of leaving,' said Karl's mother. 'It's five past twelve.'

At least she knows the time. Joseph raised himself on his elbow and looked out the window. The sun was now directly above them and the umbrella tree had drawn in its shade, leaving Karl's mother on its periphery. Anna was sitting on the other side, nodding her head, sighing heavily from time to time. Joseph wished he had been kinder to her.

'So where's that Joseph of yours?' the old woman asked. 'I'd like to meet him before we leave.'

The last thing he wanted was to meet Anna's madams. Joseph lay back on the bed and closed his eyes. Zandile.

Would they ever meet again? It was eight months since they had parted. Perhaps she thought he no longer loved her or that he had sold out. They had had so little time together. Love in dark township streets, embraces in the veld strewn with the flowers of Soweto: beer cans, cigarette boxes, paper, plastic. Groping through her layers of clothing with his trembling, uncertain hand, he had felt the soft rise of her breasts, the curve of her hips, the warmth of her thighs. By now she would have met a stronger, braver man who would know how to love a woman. A suppressed cry rose up from his depths.

'Modimo!' he shouted into the pillow, blinking away his tears. 'Modimo! Get me out of here!'

The cat leapt onto his bed and rubbed her mangy fur against his legs. He stroked her absently and breathed slowly, deliberately, until his heart beat normally again. What kind of soldier will I be if I can't even handle the fantasies of my over-heated brain? Think of Alex; think of his hardships.

'My real name,' Alex had told him one evening, 'is Rammidi Radebe, but no one except my parents ever called me that. At the mission school they called me many names, few of them complimentary. And my political friends sarcastically named me Alexander the Great, Alex for short, because I was always quoting him. He wanted to unite the Greeks in a war against the Persian empire. Only in the new era shall I decide what my name will be.'

'Who gave me my name?' Joseph had enquired shyly.

'Ellen. But I prefer Senkatana. Alex and Senkatana. By those names we'll know one another.'

Well-matched names, like Sello and Dikeledi, Crying and Tears. Dikeledi explained that there had been a death in the family when she was born, so they called her Tears. But I take the name with happiness, not with tears, she had told Joseph; I eat with an old-fashioned spoon. Old fashioned names, old fashioned people.

Until 1960 Alex and his comrades still believed that there could be a political solution to the country's problems. When the ANC was banned, and its leaders arrested or exiled, the military wing was formed: violence would now be met with violence. Alex described to Joseph their amateurish beginnings; how they had learned to load, clean, dismantle and reassemble pistols; how they had made petrol bombs.

'In the beginning we were better with spray guns, with which we painted slogans all over Johannesburg, than with real guns. Sabotage was never directed against human life, only against installations,' he said when he described his first attempt at blowing up a pylon. 'Only two of the four explosives placed at the base of the pylon went off. The pylon looked more like the leaning tower of Pisa than a target of revolutionary wrath.'

He had not talked about his time in exile. 'The less you know the better,' he had told Joseph one wintry evening when they had sat behind Motana's store warming themselves at an old brazier they had found on the rubbish heap. 'Safer for you, safer for others. The interrogators have irresistible methods for extracting information.'

After three years on the run and in hiding, Alex had slipped out of the country in 1963. During that time he had lived in different places and in various disguises, always in danger of betrayal or arrest. Ellen had remained loyal, if disgruntled.

'I understood her bitterness when I left, but there was nothing I could do about it.'

He'd had no communication with Ellen or with other members of his family for the four years he had been away, but he got news of them indirectly.

70

'Sometimes no news is better than some news,' he said wryly. 'Particularly the kind of news that dribbled through about Ellen. I had no right to expect fidelity from her. I even had no right to the jealousy and anger I suffered. I loved her,' he said, shading his eyes with his hand, 'but I'd made a choice and had to take the consequences. A close friend of mine always said that people like us shouldn't ever love or marry. These are extraordinary times and one cannot live an ordinary life.'

Yet he, Joseph, still dreamed of finishing his studies, going to university, writing poetry and marrying Zandile. With her he could even live in a village like this one. He had never liked the city. Perhaps he and other young people could return to the land, plough, sow and reap together; build schools for their children who would grow up literate, intelligent, aware of their past, in control of their future. Was that such a crazy thing to wish for, to dream of? Senkatana. How dared he call himself Senkatana when he had such ordinary dreams?

Joseph went out to the kitchen and scooped up a mug of water from the bucket. The intense sunlight blinded him and the heat beat down on his naked back. In the distance he heard the chugging of a vehicle. That would be the bus that came to the village three times a week from Pretoria, Joseph thought as he stretched himself wearily.

From the mealie patch he heard Sammy calling, 'Boetie! Boetie!' between bouts of coughing. Joseph sat down in the shade cast by the kitchen roof and waited for Sammy to appear. It would not take him long to discover that Joseph was not in the field.

'Here I am,' he said softly when Sammy emerged from the mealies looking hot and tired. 'What is it?'

'Why didn't you answer me?' Sammy said petulantly. 'I was calling and calling.'

'I'm hiding,' Joseph whispered, drawing Sammy down between his legs. 'I don't want the visitors to see me.'

'But Mmemogolo will be cross! She wants you to come and meet the visitors. She says I must tell you they are good people.'

Good people. Sello and Dikeledi were also good people. And good people are exploited people. The country was choked with such good people. What it needed was some bad people who would burn away the paralysing sickness that the good people had spread.

'Good people? Then I'll have to go. Give the cat some more milk and clean up her mess in the room,' he said, giving him a playful push in the direction of the house.

He dusted his pants as he stood up. Out of respect for his grandmother, he decided, he would put on a shirt.

TEN

People with bony bums, Louise thought as she got up from the hard chair, make good guests: they feel when it is time to go home. It was obvious that Freda did not suffer from the same anatomical deficiency. She looked as though she was settling in for the day.

'We should think of leaving,' Louise said to her. 'It's five past twelve.'

'Soon, soon,' Freda said, turning back to Dikeledi and Sello. 'You must go to the Chief . . . '

What the village needs is Freda, Louise reflected as her mother-in-law earnestly urged the old people on to action. She never gave up. She would probably inspan the Chief and make him pull a plough. Dikeledi seemed too gentle and, well yes, servile, to stand up to authority. And Sello, after thirty years of domestic servitude, had no doubt been broken in a long time ago. She imagined that their grandson, Joseph, about whom Dikeledi spoke with such pride, was yet another accepting rural black. The apple never falls far from the tree.

Louise stretched out her arms, intertwining her fingers at the nape of her neck. Her dress clung to her damp body. A hot wind blew through the umbrella tree, dislodging the remaining flowers – round, fluffy, yellow – from the grey-green foliage, sweetening the air in their fall. The flat-topped crown of the tree stood about twelve feet from the ground. The bark was dark brown, roughly fissured, and on the horizontal branches, which started to spread only a few feet from the base, were pairs of thorns: one small hooked brown thorn, and a longer thorn which was white, straight and slender. Thorns. Nature's reaction to dry conditions. She could have sprouted thorns a long time ago.

Her marriage to Tony had broken down soon after he brought Beulah home.

'Beulah's up from Cape Town to help me on a paper about the Group Areas Act. She'll be staying with us,' he announced.

Beulah was 'coloured' and would know about separate development. She was a short, dark girl with curly black hair, small-waisted, big-bottomed, with legs like a pair of hams. Bushman ancestry, Louise decided; distinct steatopygic characteristics. She also had a pert nose, long-lashed brown eyes and a slow, shy smile which Tony courted assiduously, showing off in front of her like a besotted schoolboy. Louise saw immediately that they were in love.

What she could not understand was how Tony, so fastidious about his own appearance, was not repelled by her dirty finger nails, her unkempt hair, the smell of sweat which clung to her clothes. Perhaps he thought it was all genuine working class. Tony was an admirer of everything working class though he himself could not knock a nail in straight.

He joked about his physical ineptness, blaming it on his white, Jewish, middle-class, South African origins. But never in Freda's hearing.

'Before I joined the Party, I thought Manual Labour was a Spanish dancer,' he told Beulah one evening when they were sitting at the dining-room table, their papers spread out all about them. Beulah laughed huskily. Louise was sitting on the other side of the room mending Karl's pants.

Liar! she wanted to call out. You grew up with Freda's trade union activities. You were suckled on strikes and nurtured on protest meetings. You're making that hoary joke to raise a cheap laugh. But she kept quiet; that was not the way to win Tony back.

To wrest another smile from Beulah, Tony told her about his first sabotage attempt. He had never spoken about it to Louise.

'It was a dark and stormy night,' he said, 'and two of us went out to blow up a pylon. The explosives must have got wet and only two of the four went off, tilting the bloody thing at such an angle, that it looked like the Leaning Tower of Pisa. What amateurs we were.'

Beulah had smiled sadly for his failure. Louise sighed for her invisibility. She was beginning to doubt her own existence.

She and Beulah circled óne another nervously: wife and mistress, the intruder and the threatened. Louise made tentative passes at friendship to which Beulah had begun to respond, but Tony made it quite clear that Beulah was head wife and that this was not going to be anything as comfortable as a ménage à trois.

His compulsive honesty was matched only by his insensitivity to Louise's pain and humiliation. At first Beulah had been inhibited by Louise's presence; later she ignored it. She and Tony sat at the table, gazing at one another as though they were the only beings on earth.

Look at me, Louise wanted to cry out. I'm here, I'm suffering. Don't flaunt your love. But she kept quiet. She understood that love could not be induced or dismissed. She had also learned that love was transient. So she sat back in silence.

Louise never discovered whether or not their love was transient. Two months after Tony had brought Beulah home, he was arrested, brought to trial and sentenced to life imprisonment. Some of his comrades were arrested with him, others fled. Beulah waited too long for permission to visit Tony in jail. She was banned, then house-arrested in a desolate village in the Western Cape. Five years later she left on an exit permit for London.

Louise's first prison visit had been tense and difficult. Tony looked thin, exhausted, and had dark shadows under his eyes.

'How is, how are the children?' he asked.

Beulah's name hung heavily between them, unspoken. Louise was not going to make it easy for him.

'Fine. I'm seeing someone on Tuesday about bringing the children to visit you,' she said.

'And, how are you?' he asked, a desperate note creeping into his voice.

'That's the first time you've asked in months,' she laughed bitterly. 'I'm fine. It's lonely in the house and difficult to answer the children's questions.'

'Tell them the truth,' he said brusquely.

'They're so young . . . Are they treating you all right?' she asked after a short silence.

'Physically well.'

They looked at one another. He'll have to ask, unaided, Louise decided.

'Uh, when you see that person, about the children I mean, coming here . . . Ask them to let Beulah visit me,' he blurted out.

Louise looked down at her tightly clenched fists and did not reply.

'I'm sorry, Louise,' Tony said with unexpected tenderness. 'I didn't plan it that way. It happened. Overwhelmingly. It could make all the difference to me if you asked. Try. If you ask, they might allow it. They've refused Peter.'

So he had already tried. Louise's heart constricted in an already familiar manner. It took all her willpower not to smash her handbag against the slatted glass partition and run out of the room. The prison authorities would have loved that. If she and Tony had nothing else between them, they at least shared a common hatred. She did not speak for fear of crying. With a sense of drowning, she felt her nose block with bitter suppressed tears.

'Perhaps,' she said, looking at her watch. 'The children are alone, I must go.' She turned around abruptly and walked out of the cold room.

Her interview with Major Slater the following Tuesday had been a nightmare of a different kind. She had not expected a slickly-groomed man who smelled of Brylcream and Old Spice and who wore a signet ring with a black stone on the fourth finger of his left hand.

'We're not monsters,' he assured her. Then he launched into a long monologue about his enlightened reign in the Rhodesian Prisons' Department. He smiled often, in the manner of a man who thinks he is attractive to women. 'Believe me,' he said, 'it gives me no joy to see the agony of prisoners' families. But I shall have to ask my superiors about the children's visits. We don't encourage it. Is there anything else?'

'No.' She stood up. 'Well, yes. Is my husband allowed other visitors?'

'Strictly speaking no. Only relatives of the first degree: mother, father, wife, brothers, sisters, perhaps children if they're old enough. Did you have anyone in mind?' He smiled.

The bastard knows. They probably had tapes of her fights with Tony, of Tony's love scenes with Beulah. The house had been thoroughly bugged.

'As a matter of fact, yes. An old friend of ours, Beulah Williams.'

'Beulah Williams. Of course. You know that the prisoner's lawyer has already made representations on her behalf? The request's been turned down.'

'Is there no way of getting permission?'

Slater's smile drew her in as an accomplice. He tilted back his chair and looked at her thoughtfully.

'Let's talk like adults, Mrs Buchman. We happen to know that your husband had an, er, involvement with Williams. We also know that there has been friction between you and the prisoner, that he was, in fact, contemplating divorce . . . '

He's lying. Tony had not thought of divorce. Slater was deliberately stirring up mischief.

'As I said, Mrs Buchman, we're not monsters. We understand affairs of the heart. It's a terrible shame that an attractive lady like you should be tied to Buchman. Again, the prisoner has been punished already by a life sentence, so he should at least have some choice of who visits him. If you are prepared to sign an affidavit to the effect that you and the prisoner no longer have a relationship and that you would be prepared to waive your visiting and writing privileges to a woman who had, in fact, been his common law wife for some time, I might be able to arrange something.'

Louise was stunned by his audacity. Common law wife. Beulah was coloured and they did not recognise any marriage across the colour line. She did not believe that Slater had the power to do this, but she couldn't call his bluff.

She stood up and Slater smiled as he saw her to the door.

'Think about it, Mrs Buchman. This shall remain our

little secret. Lawyers tend to ruin such things. It depends on you whether you'll be a free woman or whether you'll remain tied to a man who has caused you such pain. Let me know before your next visit to the prisoner.'

Louise cried all through that night. The next day she phoned Slater and refused his offer.

'It's up to you, Mrs Buchman,' he said amiably. 'But I think your husband will take it badly when he hears of it.'

Freda had done all the talking on the next visit to Tony. Louise answered a few questions about the children, then lapsed into silence. How did that saying go? Something about the gods granting the wishes of those whom they wished to destroy. She would now have Tony to herself for the rest of her life, sharing him with just one other woman, his mother.

When the visit ended, she and Tony looked at one another for a long time. There was no love in that look, only forlorn acceptance. In the years that followed neither of them mentioned Beulah again.

ELEVEN

He could be anything between eighteen and twenty-eight, Louise guessed when Joseph came out of the house. She couldn't tell age in Africans. It was probably an extension of that race-blindness syndrome which perceives all Chinese or Africans as looking alike.

'Joseph,' Dikeledi introduced him, 'son of my daughter Ellen.'

Louise looked at him keenly: he's been well-loved, probably by Dikeledi. African women rarely raised their own children. Joseph, she had said so proudly. In spite of the rather sullen look on his face, Louise sensed a charmed air about him. Charmed, not charming, Louise decided as Joseph acknowledged them with a slight nod as 'the Madams of Anna'.

He sat down on the doorstep next to his young brother who thrust a thick branch into his hand and whispered something in his ear. Joseph allowed himself a small smile, took a penknife out of his trouser pocket and began whittling away at the wood.

There was an unmistakable air about people who had been close to their nurturers. Louise recognised it in Joseph. Tony had it, Freddie had it, Karl did not. Her brother had it, she did not. Love was unjust. Those who deserved or needed it most did not necessarily get a fair share. Like Karl. Understanding him as she did, she felt protective, concerned, affectionate. Freddie she loved unconditionally.

Karl had been four and Freddie two when Tony went to jail. On their first and only visit, Freddie had clung to Louise, stealing shy glances at Tony. Karl had tugged at the glass slats, impatient to get to Tony.

'Open the window, Daddy,' he demanded. 'I want to be on your shoulders.'

'Not today,' Tony had answered, his face taut. Tell them the truth, he had instructed Louise after his arrest. It was harder than he imagined it would be.

'Come home also, I want you to come home!' Karl had screamed as Louise took him and Freddie out of the room. Even the warders had looked distressed.

Later that week, Louise had received a letter saying that it was undesirable to expose young children to prison conditions. She could apply again when they reached the age of sixteen.

'The punishment only begins with the sentence,' Tony had said when she read the letter to him. 'Black children often grow up without fathers,' he added when her eyes filled with tears. Louise wasn't sure if he was rebuking her or offering comfort.

Tony watched his children grow up through photographs and heard about their progress behind glass slats. When they met again, twelve years later, they were strangers to one another.

As Louise watched Joseph chip away at the wood, marvelling at his skill and his patience, she wondered if he had known his father. In repose Joseph lost his sullen look and was a handsome young man. Small well-shaped ears lay close against his shaven mahogany-brown head, and his almond eyes mirrored volatile emotions – affection for Sammy, respect tinged with pity for Sello, love for Dikeledi. When he glanced at her and Freda, she saw hostility in his eyes. He was tall and slender and his sensitive fingers handled the wood with skill and confidence. He's an artist, she thought. How can he sit in this village day after day without going crazy? He must have felt her eyes on him and he looked up. She held his proud angry look with difficulty.

Tony's black friends had also been angry, but unlike this generation, they had still believed it possible to work with whites for change. She had rarely spoken to them. When they had come to the house, Tony introduced them to her in a perfunctory manner – she rarely caught their names – and whisked them into the study. Tony's youthful error, she imagined them saying. Her humiliation was compounded when, after Beulah moved in, they greeted her warmly, embraced her and called her Sissie.

Louise had been very lonely after Tony's arrest. She even missed Beulah, in a strange sort of way. She saw none of Tony's friends. Many had fled, some had been arrested, and those who remained showed no interest in her. She took a full-time teaching job at a Jewish day school about seven minutes drive from the house and placed Karl in the kindergarten attached to it. Freddie joined him the following year.

'They'll become Jewish chauvinists,' Tony had complained. He had spoken of 'zionist imperialism' long before it became a cliche with the New Left.

'Some of my best friends – and relatives – are Jewish,' Louise had replied. She refused to move Karl to another nursery school.

She enjoyed her job as an English teacher. It was relatively well-paid and she liked the pupils and teachers. If she did have reservations, she never discussed them with Tony. Every now and again a guest speaker, with total

82

disregard for the gentile teachers on the staff, would inveigh against mixed marriage as though it were a cardinal sin, and would warn about the evils of assimilation. Even after the Holocaust, the theme ran, the goyim still seek to destroy us. Louise had been mollified by the angry reaction of most of the teachers and pupils.

'I escaped from the Afrikaner laager only to be caught up in a Jewish one,' she said to her friend Lena Goldschmidt, the art teacher at the school.

'The comparison isn't as neat as it seems,' she replied.

Lena was a German Jewess who wore loose flowing robes and heavy jewellery, especially bracelets: they hid the number tattooed on her arm. She never spoke about her experiences. All Louise knew was that between the ages of eighteen and twenty-one she had been in Auschwitz.

'How does one emerge sane from such an experience?' Louise had asked her one day.

Lena took her into her studio where she worked every day after school. Louise shuddered every time she thought of the paintings she had seen there.

'Everyone needs an emotional safety valve,' Lena had said. 'You have your poetry. Keep writing.'

Her husband Ernst was a psychoanalyst. What else should a bright Jewish boy from Vienna become, Lena had said when she introduced him to Louise. The Goldsch-midts were about ten years older than Louise and they 'adopted' her and the boys. They lived in a low, cool house on the ridge above the school. The white-washed walls were hung with paintings by South African artists, many of whom were Lena's friends; the tiled floors were covered with oriental rugs, and there was always music in the house.

'I will initiate you into the art of listening,' Ernst

Goldschmidt told Louise who expressed an interest in learning about music, 'as opposed to the habit of over-hearing. With time one's tastes change, as you will notice. In my callow youth I wept with Tchaikovsky, went heroic with Beethoven, romantic with Chopin, and travelled snowy wastes with Sibelius. Today in my dotage, I would gladly listen to nothing but Baroque.'

Louise went romantic with Chopin. Ernst was an attractive man. Once blond, he now had iron-grey hair that fell over his forehead, like Von Karajan's. His dark eyes seemed to beam into her very soul, illuminating a self she only suspected was there. In his presence, Louise felt herself becoming visible again.

'You're young, attractive and very vulnerable,' Ernst told her when he realised what was happening. 'I'm a father figure for you. And even if all the other circum-stances were right, it wouldn't work,' he said, trying to laugh her out of what he saw as an infatuation. 'Music's the acid test. Chopin stirs your soul, Baroque stirs mine. We met too late. By the time you get around to Baroque, I'll be dead. What you need is a young, vigorous man, not an old cynic like me.'

Louise did not meet any vigorous young men. The few she had met, retreated when they heard that her husband was serving a life sentence. She had not cared enough for any of them to say that her relationship with Tony had been over long before he had gone to jail.

One evening at the Goldschmidts, Louise watched Ernst glow with pride as Lena – gay, witty, the darkness of her soul locked into her studio – presided over their dinner table. She realised how deeply he loved Lena, and knew that she could not do anything to hurt either of them.

Petty bourgeois diversions, Tony had sneered when she

told him of her friendship with the Goldschmidts and their friends. Most of them had a Central European background and she was enchanted with their dedication to their cultured lives, their ability to laugh at everything, their lack of political commitment. After a while she began to evoke her own distant Huguenot origins. But after 16 June, everything fell into place for her, and she understood how deeply African she really was.

Nothing had moved or disturbed her, ever, as much as the Revolt of the Children. Tony, for all his political prescience, had not foreseen it. His revolution was to have started with the working class. But while he and his comrades languished in jail or in exile, their pamphlets and blueprints for political panaceas in shreds, the children of the black ghettoes rose in a passionate, spontaneous outburst, and faced the guns of their oppressors, armed with little more than sticks and stones.

Karl had left the country before his army call-up. I am not going to shoot down black guerillas or black children, he said. The black caddy syndrome, however, followed him into exile. It's not your struggle, some adoptive black brothers told him.

Freddie went into a different kind of exile. He withdrew into a hermit-like existence of meditation and reunciation. He too would refuse his call-up when it came, but he would not leave the country. I am a conscientious objector, he said calmly, and I'll make my stand here.

In the face of all this anguish, Louise felt bewildered and lost. All she knew was that she was of Africa and that she would never leave it. The Goldschmidts and their friends would leave one day; they had been refugees before. Months ago the talk had already been of Canada, Australia, America; they were seasoned survivors. Louise did not judge them, but her Huguenot origins ceased to interest her.

A skinny ginger cat with drooping teats and rheumy eyes came out of the house and went up to Joseph, rubbing her mangy fur against his legs, mewing hoarsely. Joseph said something to Sammy who picked her up and took her away. Freda, Dikeledi and Anna were talking about their children's school days.

'He made too much trouble in the school,' Dikeledi said of Joseph, not without pride. 'And when the teacher she's cross, they run from the village, from the school, him and Mojalefa.'

Anna moaned softly and nodded her head. Joseph did not acknowledge that he was being discussed. Perhaps he doesn't understand English, Louise thought.

'Tony always wanted to build things,' Freda sighed, 'not to blow them up. But there it is . . . '

'Mojalefa, he was not interested in the study like Joseph,' Anna said quietly. 'He just wanted to play football for Kaizer Chiefs, that's all.'

'You worry too much about him,' Freda said. 'I'm sure he'll be home soon.'

'I do not wish for him to be home,' Anna shook her head vehemently. 'When he comes, people will die. He will die. He will lie in the street like a dog and they will not let me bury him. The vultures will eat his eyes . . . ai, ai, ai!'

She began wailing so loudly that Sello, who had dropped off to sleep again, woke up. Joseph cast an angry look at her. He's not the rural black he pretends to be, Louise thought. She withdrew from the lengthening shade of the umbrella tree, distancing herself from Anna's histrionics.

Dikeledi and Freda fussed over her while Sello limped into the house to fetch a mugful of water.

Mojalefa would have been ashamed of her. Joseph dug the knife deeply into the soft wood. The vultures will eat his eyes . . . This was not the true sorrow which had forced Anna to the ground only a short while ago in the mealie field. This was an act for her white madams. He turned back to his carving, his head bent in contempt.

TWELVE

Joseph held the piece of wood at arm's length and surveyed the giraffe's head that was beginning to emerge. He had never seen a live giraffe. He had seen only the cars that passed through his great-uncle's village during the school holidays on their way to the game reserve. They had sped over the road, raising red clouds of dust that settled over the high roadside grass, on the mopane trees, and over the village children who ran into the road, their hands outstretched.

If I were a real artist, Joseph mused as he shaped the giraffe's truncated horns, I would represent our past as a big outstretched hand, a whole series of hands, culminating in the clenched fist.

There had been many clenched fists that morning when they met in the school grounds; cold chapped fists held up to the pale winter light. Zandile had stood beside him, shivering with cold and excitement. The air was electric, crackling with placards on which they had worked the previous night. 'Viva Azania!' his placard read.

He had tried, over the past few months, to recall the exact sequence of events. All he could dredge up were a few disparate images: Zandile's icy hand in his own as they moved off to join the others; the winter veld with its tall grass, dry and yellow, swaying in the cold wind; the pall of smoke over the township; the workers surging towards train and bus terminals. His mind had ceased functioning. Isolated images and sentences surfaced into consciousness but he had no coherent thoughts. His physical awareness, however, had intensified. He felt the rough wool of his sweater against his neck, the tightness of his out-grown shoes, the steel of his penknife against his cold thigh. An image of Malome Benedict flashed through his mind – tall, gaunt, wrapped in his trenchcoat as he trudged through the dry veld. The old man's words reverberated in his ears: Beware the forked lightning; the night of the fires is coming. Joseph took the knife from his trouser pocket, unsheathed it, and placed it in his blazer pocket for easier access. He smiled; he was not as free from superstition as he hoped.

He and Zandile had stood on the koppie overlooking the Phefene Junior Secondary school, watching streams of students converge on it from all directions. There were chants and laughter, clenched fists and waving banners: Down with Afrikaans! Amandla! Viva Azania! Then the police vehicles appeared, and men in camouflage uniforms jumped from the vans, holding dogs on leashes.

'I'm afraid,' Zandile had said softly.

Gripping his placard in one hand and Zandile's cold hand in the other, they ran over the rocks, through the dry grass, towards the school. The police were fanning out, surrounding the students.

'Senkatana! Here comes General Senkatana!' Mafika had shouted out in English. 'No action without Senkatana!' he jeered.

'One of their leaders,' Joseph heard a police sergeant call out in Afrikaans. 'Follow him!'

That bastard. Joseph hated Mafika even more than he hated the police who were closing in on them. Mafika had called him names since his first day at school.

'Mafika's showing off,' Joseph whispered to Zandile. 'There's a policeman with a dog behind us. Quick, push your way into the crowd, disappear. I'll shake him off. Meet me later at Mojalefa's place.'

As he turned around, he saw the policeman release the dog with an urgent command. Joseph instinctively pulled the knife out of his pocket. As the dog leapt at him, Joseph drove the knife into his throat, feeling the steel crunch through fur, flesh and bone. There was a roar of approval from his fellow students as, baptised in blood, he was pulled into the thick of the crowd, away from the writhing dog and his stupified handler. After that there was no turning back; he had become a reluctant hero.

Suddenly the atmosphere changed. The laughter and the chanting gave way to angry shouts and screams of pain as the police opened fire. Sirens pierced the air and the whole township seemed ablaze. Black smoke spiralled into the pale sky while helicopters hovered overhead, dropping reinforcements and tear gas.

Joseph could not recall the exact chain of events that brought him and his group to his own neighbourhood towards dusk. All he knew was that his hands were cut and bleeding, that they had left behind burnt-out vehicles and smashed windows, and that he stank of petrol and of the liquor they had emptied into the streets. There had been no heroics; contact with the police was avoided.

'Bullets make dead!' Mojalefa had shouted to his friends who urged confrontation. 'We'll fight them when we're armed with more than stones and sticks. In the meantime, hit and waai!'

'Burn, burn, burn!' Mafika had shrieked. 'Death to all shebeens and their queens!'

Joseph stepped back involuntarily; they were standing outside his own house. The students around him picked up stones and he heard the shattering of glass.

'Hey you, hero, Senkatana! Why do you stand back?'

Mafika bawled, his eyes rolling. Everyone turned to look at Joseph.

As Joseph picked up a stone, his heart grew cold: he wished he could die. He remembered the blare of the music, the smell of liquor, the vomit on the floor. He thought of Lucky and the fat-folds of his neck; he remembered the creaking of bedsprings, the ugly laughter. But nothing gave him the strength to lift up his arm and throw the stone.

'Coward! Hypocrite!' Mafika shouted hoarsely, rushing through the front gate towards the door. 'Petrol! Petrol and matches! Burn! Burn!'

There had been no sign of life from the house. Joseph prayed that Ellen was not home. It was quite dark now and all around them fires were shooting into the smoke-filled sky. The air was thick with tear gas smoke and with the smell of burning rubber. People ran through the streets with their faces covered. Explosions, screams and sirens were a constant backdrop to the chaotic scenes of destruction. Just as Mafika was pouring petrol onto the front door, it flew open and Ellen appeared, dishevelled, eyes round with fear and fury.

'Voetsek!' she shouted, pushing Mafika off the step. 'Voetsek! I never made you trouble. Go away, go away!' she screamed at the others. Then she saw Joseph at the back of the crowd, a stone in his hand. Her mouth quivered and she let out a long, tortured wail.

Joseph did not see Alex approaching. It was only when the crowd began to disperse that he saw Alex's burly figure move among them, urging them quietly but with authority to leave immediately. Ellen was sitting in the middle of her small garden, rocking herself and wailing. She had not yet seen Alex.

There was a moment of complete silence as the crowd

melted away. It was as if the whole township were taking a deep breath before the final explosion. Alex helped Ellen to her feet. She looked up at him. Large tears ran down her face as he took her into his arms and held her against him, his head resting on hers. Joseph remained outside the gate, the stone in his hand.

'They'll be back,' Alex said as he released her. 'Pack a few things and I'll take you to Auntie Mary. Wait there a while, then go to your mother till this blows over. And you,' he said, walking towards Joseph, 'you have much to learn.' He knocked the stone out of his hand, then raised his hand as though to hit him.

'I wasn't going to throw it, I couldn't,' Joseph said.

Alex looked at him, then lowered his arm.

'We'll talk later,' he said, 'after I've taken your mother to Auntie Mary.'

It was midnight before he returned.

'Mojalefa has left,' he told Joseph, 'But Zandile is still here. You can see her for a few minutes before she goes.'

That was the last time he had seen Zandile, with her blackened eyes, missing tooth, and swollen face. Then Alex drove him to the village.

'You must stay there until we can arrange safe transport. It may take months,' he warned. 'The watch on the borders will tighten.'

'Why can't I go with Zandile, with Mojalefa?'

'No time, no place,' Alex answered firmly.

Joseph felt too tired to argue; he found it difficult to speak. His whole body ached and he was shivering. Alex covered him with a heavy overcoat that he took from the back seat.

'You students are brave, militant, imaginative,' he said, 'but that's not enough to break the System. You must have the support of the people, of the workers. It will come, but the time is not yet ripe.'

'They're afraid to risk their jobs, to lose their wages,' Joseph said. 'We'll have to do it alone.'

'You can't, believe me. You'll be crushed, like cock-roaches. The townships can easily be sealed off by a small detachment of police. You must have the people with you. You can't do it alone.'

Joseph was silent. Mafika was right. The ANC had grown soft in exile.

'Black consciousness people say,' Joseph began.

'Black consciousness is the product of a siege culture,' Alex said impatiently. 'A necessary stage but exclusive, dogmatic, short-sighted.'

'I don't know what to do, what to think,' Joseph's voice rose on a desperate note. 'We need to act now, before we too are broken.'

He had expected Alex to react angrily. Instead, he had reached out and gripped Joseph's arm.

'Sleep now. This is not the time for talking,' he said quietly.

Joseph covered himself with the overcoat and lay back, watching Alex's profile emerge out of darkness against the pale dawn sky.

Eight months had passed since that night. Mafika and his friends – or perhaps it had been another group – had returned the next day and thrown a petrol bomb into Ellen's house. It was completely burned out. Ellen had stayed at the village for a while, then returned to Soweto. She and Joseph had not exchanged one word all the time she had been in the village. She and everyone else – except Alex, Dikeledi and Sello, perhaps – believed that it was he who had instigated the attack on her house.

THIRTEEN

'Sing me some songs and I'll tell you your history,' the old woman was saying. 'Songs, and the bitter ironic jokes we Jews tell against ourselves, that's what has helped us survive. Some say religion did. Perhaps. Just listen to your people out there on the river bank. Religion certainly keeps them going. People need something bigger than themselves to believe in, but I don't think it should be religion. What do you think, young man?' She turned to Joseph, who had hoped that if he sat quietly, carving the giraffe's head, he might make himself invisible to the white visitors.

'Religion is dangerous,' he was surprised into saying. 'It takes people's minds off the real problems.'

'Smart chap,' the old lady said, raising her eyebrows.

Karl's mother sat up straight and looked at him. Joseph turned back to his carving. They wouldn't have been more surprised if he'd turned into a giraffe. What had they expected him to say? Hau, Medem, I not understand what the missis say?

'Listen to the songs,' Freda said to Joseph, 'and you won't need history books. The poor and the oppressed sing the same songs all over the world, in different languages. Would you like to hear a Yiddish song?'

Dikeledi clapped her hands, Sello grinned broadly, and Anna suppressed her sobs. Karl's mother, Joseph observed, looked exasperated.

Throwing back her head she began to sing in a deep, sad voice.

94

Un du akarst, un du zeist,
Un du hammerst, un du neist . . .

Joseph was amazed that such beautiful sounds could pour out of that ugly, flabby throat. He could not understand the words, but the pain was palpable.

'That song,' the old woman said, wiping her eyes, 'was about workers who till the soil but own no land, who sew for the rich but themselves wear rags, who build palaces but live in hovels. You see what I mean about the similarities? And if you think that's sad, just wait till I sing you a love song!' She laughed. 'But even in those days new kinds of song were being sung – songs of hope, of revolution. What about your songs? My friend Mofolo tells me you have songs for everything, for work, for being born, for dying, for feasts and for funerals.'

'We got plenty songs,' Dikeledi assented. 'But a long time now we forget to sing. Only my big uncle, the doctor, he knows the songs. But we got plenty chech hymns. The young ones,' she nodded towards Joseph, 'they make new songs from old hymns. The predikant he does not like it. Sing please a song, Joseph.'

Joseph looked up angrily from his carving, shaking his head. What did she want him to sing? Amabhulu Zinzinja? They had all gone mad, sitting there in the heat, under a tree in the middle of the African veld, listening to songs about Jews in Russia. He wanted to get up and run.

Sammy was leaning on Joseph's knee, his mouth open, breathing heavily, unevenly. Every now and again he suppressed a cough. The clinic could do nothing for him; he must be taken to town. Joseph drew him closer, shooing a fly off his face. Perhaps he should speak to Anna about it. She had cast off her betrayed-mother act and was now beating time to the old woman's song.

95

Joseph leaned back against the door and shut his eyes. The sun beat down fiercely, relieved only by a soft dry wind which wafted the smell of the músú's flowers towards him. The old woman's voice mingled with the hum of insects, the rustling of the dry grass and the sound of the bus chugging along the road. Then a shadow fell between him and the sun.

He opened his eyes: Malome Benedict stood there, looking down at him, his neck hunched into his shoulders, his face half-hidden in the raised collar of his trenchcoat.

The singing had stopped. Only the steady buzz of flies and bees, punctuated by an occasional birdcall, broke the silence. Dikeledi's breath came in quick chesty rasps. This was the first time Malome Benedict had shown himself to strangers since his return from the war more than thirty years ago. A few seconds passed before Joseph realised that Benedict's hand, cracked and calloused, the nails uncut, was stretched out towards him. Joseph handed him the unfinished giraffe's head and the penknife. Benedict sat down next to him. The rough fibre of his coat, encrusted with the dust of the veld and far-off places, rubbed against Joseph's bare arm, and a smell of woods-moke and khaki weed emanated from its rigid folds.

There were tears in Dikeledi's eyes as she turned to the other women.

'My son Benedict,' she said.

'Sing, Mokgotse, sing more,' he said in a deep voice, hoarse from disuse. Then with deft movements, he began reworking the head of the giraffe.

Joseph watched the incredulous look on the old woman's face change into a smile.

'This song,' she said to Benedict, 'is in Hebrew, the language of my people who have returned to the land of our ancestors. I myself don't understand the words, but I know it's about hope and joy.'

Karl's mother had also been startled by Malome Benedict's appearance. She stared at him, but Benedict seemed unaware of her presence. As he listened to the old woman's song, tears streamed down his rutted cheeks.

Joseph stood up. They were all bewitched. Sing, Benedict says, and the old woman sings, piercing his cloak of darkness, exorcising his ghosts. Rejected by the gods, in retreat from people, there he sits, the prophet of doom, weeping and sighing as she sings her strange songs. They came in from the veld, these white women with their songs and their tales, casting spells of false hope. Lies, all of it lies. Only the struggle is real; the evil must be burned out of the land. The old witch can't sing herself out of that, nor can the younger one pay her debt with her pain. Joseph's breath caught on a suppressed sob as he strode into the house. These whites colonised everything, even the martyrdom and the suffering.

He lay down on the bed and the cat jumped up beside him, purring wetly against his leg. Only animals forget, have no memory for past hurts. Give a cat a saucer of milk, and she'll forget her dead litter. He wouldn't let himself forget: his hatred was his strength.

FOURTEEN

Louise had never before encountered such an apparition. He looked like a ghost, a very smelly ghost, that was condemned to walk the earth forever, finding no place to rest. His feet were shod in car-tyre sandals and dark ragged trousers hung out from under a soil-encrusted trenchcoat. Her father had had a coat like that with shiny brass buttons, his rank spelled out by the pips on his shoulder. She remembered the rough prickly texture so well. Some ex-soldier must have given this scruffy black man – my son, Benedict, Dikeledi had said sadly – that coat.

Louise looked carefully at that part of his face which was visible behind the raised collar. His features were smudged by his blackness, his peppercorn hair was white, and his voice echoed like Hamlet's father's ghost in the Olivier film. She watched his hands move deftly over the carving with sure strokes, recognising in the skilled movements the teacher of the young man, Joseph.

A sudden panic flowed over her, a fear that she would never get away from this village; that an invisible band was enclosing the group under the umbrella tree, binding them together forever. She got up quickly, at about the same time that Joseph went into the house, picked up her bag and walked towards the gate. The ants once again swarmed over her feet and climbed up her legs. She brushed them off with quick nervous strokes, then hesitated before she opened the gate: she had not said goodbye. She looked back at the umbrella tree.

Freda had finished her song and was preparing to leave. After shaking hands with Dikeledi and Sello, she turned to the man in the trenchcoat. He was wiping wood chips off the carving. Holding it at arm's length, he turned it critically this way and that. He put both the knife and the carving into the outstretched hand of the young boy who had been sitting quietly at his side. He got up with difficulty from the step and walked up to Freda, his shoulders once again hunched up, his face half-hidden in the upturned collar of his coat.

'The night of the fires is coming,' he said in his sepulchral voice. He turned away abruptly and walked out of the enclosure. It gave Louise some satisfaction to see the startled look on Freda's face as she stared after him.

In the distance Louise heard the chugging of a vehicle. She turned towards the road and saw a bus heaving over the sand road, in the direction of town. And coming towards the house, the tall grass hiding the lower part of his body she saw a familiar figure. Far from feeling reassured, the very familiarity reawakened her feeling of panic. Charlie. His appearance, she felt, was not fortuitous; the gods were staging a drama.

Louise shook off her chilling sense of foreboding. This was Charlie's birthplace, after all, this village submerged in a sea of dry grass. If anyone were a stranger, it was she. Charlie's family no doubt lived here, as Anna's did. The sun, the silence, the isolation and the heat were affecting her. She lifted her head and drew back her shoulders, breathing deliberately, evenly, in an effort to regain her composure.

'Good afternoon, Madam,' Charlie said cheerfully.

There had always been a slightly ironic note in his voice when he spoke to her, even when he had been dead drunk.

Louise, against her will, responded in a voice her pious brother Andre would have envied. She felt her ancestors close in on her, drawing her into an invisible laager.

'Good afternoon, Charlie,' she said.

'I am surprised to see the Madam here, in this forgotten village.'

'Not more surprised than I am to see you, Charlie,' she replied, tears of impotence smarting her eyes. The mocking gods were having a field day; she seemed incapable of choosing her own words. 'And so sober too.'

Charlie laughed. 'Yes, the Madam never did like my drinking. You have brought Anna to visit her mother?'

'We are still looking for Mojalefa. He disappeared from Soweto almost at the same time as you did.'

A veil seemed to descend over Charlie's bloodshot eyes. He might be sober now, Louise thought, but his eyes bear the signs of the habitual drunk.

Without another word, she walked towards the umbrella tree whose shadow had lengthened even further to the east.

'It's time to leave,' Freda said to her.

'I'm surprised you've noticed,' Louise replied.

Dikeledi and Sello greeted Charlie with great warmth. Anna ejected a stream of what Louise imagined was invective as she walked away to the furthest corner of the enclosure. Everyone talked at once: the old people in conciliatory tones, first to Charlie then to Anna; Anna shrieked angrily, and Charlie spoke in a calm explanatory voice.

During a short lull in the argument, Louise went up to Dikeledi and Sello.

'It was nice to meet you and to talk to you,' she said, wondering suddenly whether she shouldn't have given them some money. There was a five rand note in her bag but she couldn't bring herself to take it out there and then. She would send them a present by post. 'Anna,' she said, 'we'll wait for you in the car. I'd like to leave soon. Freddie is coming to visit this afternoon.'

'I am coming now,' Anna replied, not moving from the broken-down fence where it was held up by the old donkey cart. 'I have nothing to say to this rubbish. This place is too small for me and him.'

Dikeledi and Sello saw them to the gate, leaving Anna and Charlie locked in verbal battle.

'We will come again,' Freda promised. 'There is so much to talk about, so many songs to sing.'

Without me, Louise thought as she sank into the driver's seat with a sigh of relief. She felt raw and exposed, in need of another skin.

'Intriguing, most intriguing,' was all Freda said as she got into the car, her eyebrows drawn together.

Joseph sat up when he heard a new voice in the courtyard, followed by an abusive outburst from Anna. Charlie, father of Mojalefa; Charlie the drunk, of whom Mojalefa had been so desperately ashamed; Charlie the failed revolutionary about whom Alex had nonetheless spoken with compassion. I'd trust Charlie drunk more than many others sober, he had told Joseph.

There was a lull in the shouting when the two white women said goodbye and were taken to the gate by his grandparents. Then Anna turned on her husband with a burst of self-righteous anger.

'You rubbish, you. Are you not ashamed to show yourself to decent people? To run off like that and leave me with the burden. And your very own children, each and every one . . .'

This was followed by a recital of her virtues and his vices. Charlie bent his head before the storm of words, nodding assent, silent. It was only when Dikeledi and Sello returned from seeing off the women that he straightened up and smiled.

'Ho, Charlie,' Sello said mischievously, 'you've grown taller. The last time I saw you, you were shorter, bent over, seeking a piece of earth on which to lay down your head. Have you lost your thirst?'

'I still drink, Ntate Mogolo, but for companionship with my brothers, not to kill pain. And only on weekends, a little.'

'When a cow gives birth to a donkey he'll stop drinking,' Anna shouted from the gate.

'Hear him out, daughter of my friend,' Dikeledi urged. Anna stood with her back to them, muttering angrily.

'Where have you been all this time, Charlie?' Dikeledi asked. 'We did not know if you were alive or dead. But you did send money, did he not, Anna?'

'Enough to feed a cat for a week,' Anna answered. 'One with a small appetite.'

Charlie shrugged. 'When the children of the ghettoes rose to face the guns, the dogs and the hippos, I felt so ashamed of my life that I didn't know what to do. I had to go where no one knew me, where I could begin at the beginning. So I went to the mines in Rustenburg, underground with my unfortunate brothers. And there I learned about work, about brotherhood, about sharing hardships.'

'Brotherhood!' Anna retorted, swinging around. 'You always knew about brotherhood, especially the brotherhood of the shebeens. What you never knew about was fatherhood.'

'There is a strong connection there, my most abused wife,' Charlie said. Joseph could have sworn there was an ironic note in his voice but the contrite tone reasserted itself as he went on. 'I stopped feeling sorry for myself and I listened to what my brothers could tell me of their lives, and they listened to what I could tell them about the world outside the compounds; how they could help themselves change their lives, and many other things.'

'And now,' Anna asked, watching Charlie carefully, 'are you going back to your mine brotherhood?'

'For the moment. I do not yet know what the future holds. But I will continue to send you money. I understand your troubles.'

'You should! You made them!' Anna said, walking out of the courtyard with her head held high. She got into the car with the other women and they drove away.

'Ntate Mogolo,' Charlie turned to Sello. 'Joseph is here in the village with you. I want very much to speak with him. Where can I find him?'

Modimo! Another one! Joseph withdrew from the window. Charlie was the last person in the world he wanted to speak to. In his chastened mood he too was probably trying to find Mojalefa.

A few seconds later Charlie came into the room. He looked at Joseph, his eyes glowing with pride.

'From Alex to Senkatana,' he said in a deep soft voice.

Joseph came towards Charlie, trembling with excitement. Charlie grasped his hands firmly in his own.

'He trusts me again, son of my friend. He trusts me again. He says ready for the journey. He will meet you where the path turns onto the road, just after twelve tonight. He will be waiting for you.'

'I will be there.' Joseph could hardly breathe. His voice sounded strange to him, as though it were coming from a long distance. 'But first I must dig the well for the old people. There is still time.'

'And I must go visit my old people. It is many years since we have seen one another,' Charlie said, following Joseph out of the house.

Dikeledi and Sello were moving the chairs from under the umbrella tree, whose shadow was drawing towards the fence. Joseph shaded his eyes as he watched the white car bump over the path through the long grass in the direction of the sand road that led out of the village. Tonight, where the path meets the road. Joseph shivered slightly.

'I am going to fetch the pick, to dig the well,' he said to Dikeledi.

'Is there time?' Dikeledi looked at him steadily.

'There is time,' Joseph replied.

'Come back soon,' Dikeledi said softly, touching him lightly with her fingertips as he walked past. 'There is much work to be done.'

Joseph nodded and set off in the direction of Malome Benedict's shack.

Taking Shelter by Jessica Anderson

Beth seems caught in a spell cast by charming, witty Miles. She wears the lovely, pale wools he selects for her and says he shields her from the world. But Miles's reluctance to become intimate leaves Beth full of suspicions . . . and yearnings. When she meets Marcus, who is so urgent and direct, so different from Miles, her world explodes into passionate fulfillment. Surrounding Beth are her brash, sexually adventurous cousin, Kyrie; Nita, Marcus's mother – earthy, ebullient, mourning the defection of her man; and Juliet, who calls herself Miles's spare godmother and continually ponders her own dreams while making everyone else's come true. All are seeking their places in an uncertain world.

In an era when there are no rules about the age, gender, or the faithfulness of lovers; when families are scattered and marriage is optional; when the threat of AIDS lurks in the background of every relationship, these people seek permanence in a mural on a wall, in a treasured photograph, or in their own recollections. Yet their moments of tenderness and their tentative quests for continuity and love draw them together. Their story is told with the keen perception, the wit, and the emotional truth that characterize all of Jessica Anderson's work.

White Light by James McQueen

On 27 January 1945, Tony Caramia walked free from Auschwitz. More than forty years later, he is the tough and restless owner of a successful building business in Australia about to visit Thailand.

By chance, he sights a German guard from the wartime camp, reviving questions and feelings which have long haunted him. Issues of justice, responsibility and guilt emerge in the cat-and-mouse game that follows. Both men are forced to reckon with their past and their choices for the future against a backdrop of the people and landscape of Thailand.

My Father's Moon by Elizabeth Jolley

Vera is young, awkward and naive.

As schoolgirl, she has her sheltered idealism, her Quaker boarding-school education, and the warm, enveloping security of her parents.

As student nurse at the large military hospital during the war, her transition to womanhood – and victim to more experienced players – is rapid, painful and disastrous.

And as unmarried mother she flees, from the nagging tension of her home and the gossipy stares of the hospital, to Fairfields, a place of poetry, music and of people with interesting lives and ideas. Quickly she learns it is otherwise.

Yet, for Vera, always there is the moon – her companion, comforter, and the unbreakable link with her father . . .

Avenue of Eternal Peace by Nicholas Jose

After forty years of communist rule, the ancient civilisation of China, newly exposed to western influences, is in a state of vigorous contradiction. Enter Wally Frith, a leading cancer specialist, who travels from the gritty frozen north to the tranquil lakes and mountains of the south, looking for answers.

As he fights through a maze of bureaucracy and subterfuge, Wally falls in with people whose lives reflect the diversity of contemporary Peking: a model, shady traders, a basketballer, students, a dissident artist and a band of eccentric westerners.

Finally, Peking opera turns to a passionate drama for freedom and democracy, when thousands of Chinese students occupy the grey streets of the capital.

PENGUIN – THE BEST AUSTRALIAN READING

It's Raining in Mango by Thea Astley

One family traced from the 1860s to the 1980s: from Cornelius to Connie to Reever, who was last seen heading north.

Cornelius Laffey, an Irish-born journalist, wrests his family from the easy living of nineteenth-century Sydney and takes them to Cooktown in northern Queensland where thousands of diggers are searching for gold in the mud. The family confronts the horror of Aboriginal dispossession – Cornelius is sacked for reporting the slaughter. His daughter, Nadine, joins the singing whore on the barge and goes upstream, only to be washed out to sea.

The cycles of generations turn, one over the other. Only some things change. That world and this world both have their Catholic priests, their bigots, their radicals. Full of powerful and independent characters, this is an unforgettable tale of the other side of Australia's heritage.

Smyrna by Tony Maniaty

In 1922, the great Mediterranean seaport of Smyrna is ablaze: the Greeks are forced from Asia Minor in defeat. Among the refugees is Theo Tekaros, whose long journey ends in Australia. 'I was a lost soul; you'd better believe it . . . ' He meets Trixie at a wartime dance, and falls in love.

Sixty years later, their son Harry, a radio journalist deserted by his wife, heads back to Greece and Turkey in search of his father's beginnings, the past. A perpetual beginner, he is captivated by two women: an elderly bookseller in Constantinople and a Greek theatre actress. Like a latter-day Ulysses blown miles off course, Harry falls in love too. But the fabric of truth is delicate, he discovers, and mysteries abound on this planet of possibilities.

PENGUIN – THE BEST AUSTRALIAN READING

Spider Cup by Marion Halligan

Elinor leaves her husband suddenly and goes to France, to the village of Sévérac-le-Château. There she ponders the lives of other women. In the seventeenth century a wife is murdered for faithlessness; in the early twentieth century a woman embroiders sheets for a trousseau never needed; in the 1980s a successful pediatrician may or may not know what her husband is up to.

Elinor's process of transformation – from a wife to a self – is written with subtlety and humour. The journey she undertakes is more than a journey of the flesh.

Out of the Line of Fire by Mark Henshaw

To an Australian writer visiting Heidelberg, the brilliant young philosophy student Wolfi is a compelling character. From the start, the details of Wolfi's life are curious – from his inquisitorial father and passionate mother to the grandmother who pays for his sexual initiation with a prostitute and to his connections with the outlandish rogue Karl.

As we are lured by Wolfi's obsession into the mysterious and erotic maze of this novel, we find nothing is as it appears.

What in fact is fact and what in fiction is fiction?